HEMLOCK SOAMES AND

THE WATERHORSE

HEMLOCK SOAMES AND THE WATERHORSE

S M KEMMETT

The Word Tailor

HEMLOCK SOAMES AND THE WATERHORSE

 A catalogue record for this
book is available from the
National Library of Australia

ISBN: 978-0-6486500-0-3

Also available separately as eBook

This book is written in British English.
Printed in Australia.
Typeset in Times Roman 10pt.

Published by The Word Tailor.
www.smkemmettwordtailor.wordpress.com

For my mother, Audrey, who encouraged me to write.
In loving memory of my father, Michael,
who encouraged me to read.
And of my mentor, Pam, who encouraged me to do both.

CONTENTS

HEMLOCK SOAMES AND
THE WATERHORSE

CHAPTER ONE

The front door closed with a comforting click. Hermia Barrington paused on her friend's portico, and took a deep, calming breath. She relaxed her shoulder muscles, feeling the knots loosen. This had been the last Call on her list and her social duty was done for the day.

An airship droned overhead. She glanced up, beyond the roofs of the row of Georgian townhouses and the occasional mansion, at the shiny mechanical beetle hovering in the overcast sky. Its silver outline, enveloped in steam, was nearly lost against the rain clouds. She screwed up her nose. How did her acquaintances cope with the buzzing annoyance? Fortunately, the flight path did not venture near her house.

A light mizzle drifted downwards. She had not thought to bring an umbrella; it had been such a bright morning. Now the chill wind stung her cheeks. She crossed the footpath to her waiting carriage.

"Home, please, Rogers," she instructed her coachman.

Her footman held the door open for her. Once safely ensconced, she leaned back into the upholstered seat. At least she need pay no more Calls today. She let out a slow, deep breath, and let her socially-expected smile slip away. No more small-talk. No more kindly-meant advice to listen to. Or unkind insinuations. No more pretending.

The horses fidgeted and snorted, then started south along Baker Street, towards the park. Towards home.

Home, where the heart is... but her heart was with Elias, and he was not at home. She clutched her bag, her knuckles pale. She would return to a half-empty house, that was all.

She closed her eyes; a tear slid from under her long gold-blonde eyelashes. She felt in her reticule for her lace-edged handkerchief.

She pressed her lips together, to stop them from trembling. *Stop it, you silly girl.* Elias had written he would be home within the week. But that had been almost three weeks ago. Three weeks! Her throat was tight; she swallowed. Had he gotten lost? Or been injured?

As she fumbled in her bag her fingers brushed a much-folded letter. Elias had sent it two years ago, telling her of a Himalayan avalanche that buried his expedition alive. She let her fingers linger on its folds. Where *was* he now? The tear splashed onto the pale blue and grey silk of her dress. The sombre colours echoed her mood, but she wasn't in mourning. Not yet. She missed Elias dreadfully – but she had faith he would return. He *would*. She snapped her purse shut.

Enough tears. She scrubbed them away with the handkerchief, then tucked the linen scrap into her sleeve.

She stared out through the carriage window. Middle class sightseers stood on corners, studying maps; servants bustled on errands. Most of the carriages that passed them were not privately owned, but hackneys for hire.

Fashionable London was deserted; there were only one or two balls left in the Season. Most of society had already relocated to the country. Hermia, herself, had already sent half of her servants on ahead to Barrington Hall, but she had no plans to leave town yet. Not before Elias returned.

The carriage drew up to the curb outside her terraced house, opposite Ennismore Gardens. Hermia alighted. The footman sprinted ahead of her up the tiled steps, to open the front door as she approached. Rogers drove off around the corner to the Mews.

The door opened to sounds of a kerfuffle inside the hall; scrapes and bumps followed by her house maid's voice issuing instructions. Whatever was Hannah doing? Hermia stepped inside to investigate. Stained glass lead-light windows threw patches of colour onto the wallpaper and floor of the entrance hall. Hannah and the boot boy struggled to move a steamer trunk upstairs. It bumped the octagonal aquarium. The glass shook and glinted in the sunlight, earning them a reproachful look from Elias's pet axolotl.

"Hannah? What is this?" asked Hermia as she slipped off her rain-damp gloves.

"Beg pardon, madam." Hannah hurriedly lowered her end of the trunk to the floor, nodding for the boy to do likewise. They turned to face their mistress. The lad bowed and Hannah executed a polite bob. She tucked a wayward strand of hair under her cap and smiled.

"Miss Hermia, the master's home... Safe and sound!"

Hermia's heart raced. "Oh!"

She bit her lip, to suppress her smile. She mustn't make an exhibition of herself in front of the servants.

"Where is Mr. Barrington, Hannah?" she asked calmly, as she removed her hat.

"He's in the Parlour, madam."

"Thank you." Hermia handed hat and gloves to Hannah, took a deep breath and ignored her pounding heart as she strolled across the hall and opened the Parlour door.

The door clicked closed behind her, shutting out the servants. Eli stood by the newly-lit fire, warming his bare hands. He turned.

"Hemmy, my darling!" he said.

Hemmy ran across the room and threw herself into his arms. His lips as he kissed hers were warm. She slipped her fingers between his. He had not been in long: his coat sleeves were still cold and bedewed by the rain. She frowned.

"Dearest, you're frozen," she murmured. "Have you rung for tea?"

A knock came at the door. Hemmy separated from her husband and waited. Hannah entered, carrying a steaming teapot and a plate of cake. She placed the tray on the table and hesitated.

"Please, ma'am," she murmured. "There's no dinner ordered."

So there wasn't, Hemmy remembered. She hadn't expected Elias to arrive tonight; she'd only requested a cold collation to be served to her in her room. Well, with a few additions, it would suffice.

"Send out for two or three hot made dishes, Hannah. The master and I will have High Tea here in the Parlour, where it's warm."

Eli shivered.

Hemmy folded her warm hand around his cold one. "And let Matthews know Mr Barrington requires a hot bath before we eat."

"Yes, ma'am," Hannah bobbed a curtsey and withdrew.

Hemmy led Eli to the table, poured him a cup of tea, and sliced him a generous serve of cake.

"You don't deserve this, you know."

"I don't?"

"It's not done to leave a bride alone for so long. The neighbours will talk." Hemmy withheld the cake from him.

"How can I make amends?" he asked.

She raised an eyebrow and relinquished the cake.

He drew his chair up to the table and his cup towards him.

Wind rattled the window and rain slapped against the glass. Eli sipped his tea and sighed.

"So, did you find it?" she asked him. Grinning, Elias nodded.

He took a small box from his pocket, tipped several small, flat objects onto Hemmy's palm. They shone and glittered in shades of green and blue and teal.

"Dragon scales?" she asked.

He nodded. "A mother and four dragonets: The Welsh Green."

"I knew you would." She rolled them over in her palm. "Tell me..."

"Later," he said, and kissed her.

CHAPTER TWO

The rain had ceased by morning. The afternoon sun struggled through the tall windows of Elias's Gentleman's club. The low murmur of masculine conversation in one corner of the wood-panelled room failed to disturb the surrounding silence. The fragrance of fine cigars filled the air.

Elias folded back the page of his newspaper. It rustled softly. His eyes skimmed over the print, stopped if anything caught his interest, moved on. They lingered over one paragraph.

Ah, now, there was something...

To be Sold by Private Auction
Articles of property of the late Mr. Alexander McGregor, Esquire,
from his residence near Slochd Lochan will be sold at
Christie's Auction House, St. James's,
on the 8th day of August 1894, at 2 p.m. precisely.

Elias ran his eyes down the lots; there were still one or two items wanting for their house; and, of course, books. A soft sound at his elbow made him look up. The waiter stood with a tray with his drink upon it.

"Your usual, Mr Barrington?"

"Ah, thank you, Charles." Elias took the proffered glass.

An auction item caught his eye: he reached inside his jacket for a notebook but failed to find his pencil. He frowned. Of course, he'd needed a graphite rod for his experiment yesterday and his silver propelling pencil-lead had filled the need admirably. It was still on his work bench at home. *Blast.*

"I say, you there…" The occupant of the leather armchair opposite Elias gestured to Charles with an imperious right hand; the left, Elias noticed, was twitching in irritation. "My drink?"

"Yes, Sir," Charles looked perplexed. "If Sir would just remind me?"

Edward Fox-Torrington – for that's who it was, Elias realised – sighed exaggeratedly and told Charles again.

"Whisky. The good stuff. Islay, Glenturret."

Elias hid his smile behind his paper. It was the same drink Lord Fox-Torrington always ordered, and Charles knew it. The waiter's face seemed quite innocent as he offered Elias a pencil, tucked his tray under his arm and withdrew.

"Damnable cheek," Fox-Torrington muttered.

Elias ignored him. He scribbled the auction details into his notebook, quaffed his drink, placed the empty glass on the low table between the armchairs and sprang from his seat. This could be it, if it was the genuine article. This could get him noticed by the Royal Society…

The door closed behind Elias with a decorous swish.

Charles watched Fox-Torrington out of the corner of his eye, as he collected used glasses.

Fox-Torrington picked up the discarded newspaper, examined it, and smiled. His fingers rustled amongst the leaves of the potted aspidistra by the table.

Charles moved to the mantel and picked up one more glass.

Fox-Torrington retrieved a small, curlicued, silver box from the planter, replaced it with another, and slipped the first into his pocket. He scanned the room, straightened his waistcoat and left.

Charles glanced at the newspaper before refolding it. He eyed the door as it shut behind Fox-Torrington, and frowned. He could understand the gentleman's interest in the auction, but what was that little box? This would bear investigation.

He picked up his tray and made his way towards the aspidistra.

Lord Fox-Torrington alighted from the hansom cab and ran up his marble front steps; the door opened as he approached. He handed his silver topped walking stick and his top hat to the butler.

"Has Cook packed the hamper I ordered?" he asked

"Yes, M'lord. It's all ready," replied the butler.

"Have Nellie bring it up."

Fox-Torrington continued up the grand staircase. Once upstairs he went to his room and locked the door. He pulled off his tie, discarded his collar and studs on the top of the chest of drawers, along with his kid gloves, and flopped onto the bed, wrinkling the silk bed cover.

The room boasted no vegetal Morris wallpaper, but retained the light paintwork that echoed the taste of previous residents. He preferred it to the heavy look currently fashionable in furnishing, anyway. A cluttered room meant a cluttered mind.

The mantelpiece clock chimed four.

He sighed; he should probably make a move. A 'gentleman' did not keep a lady waiting. He sat up, stood and walked towards his dressing room.

The two main bedchambers were once discreetly connected by their dressing rooms into a suite. Now the other room was draped in brown Holland against the dust, and locked.

He entered the dressing room, approached the far wall and triggered its hidden locking mechanism. A section of the wall sprang out two inches. He slid open the secret door, and entered.

Nellie had lit a gas lamp and laid out the clothes, as requested, but had not yet delivered the food hamper. He checked his pocket watch and smiled. She wouldn't be long.

He removed the compact silver box he'd retrieved from the aspidistra pot from his pocket and set it on the dressing table. He pressed a concealed catch; a secret drawer within the table slid open without a noise. Reaching inside, he retrieved a set of small tools.

Handling the delicate lid with especial care, he opened the box. Inside was a complex arrangement of clockwork, magnets, and cogs. He extracted a cylindrical coil of fine metal wire, flipped it, then threaded it back into the device. A small ornate gas fitting attached neatly to the side of the box and clicked into place, providing a flower-like trumpet. He grinned at the ingenious device, and, clasping a tiny key on his watch chain, inserted it into the opposite side of the gadget and wound it several times. The box whirred with each turn.

He held the little recording gadget close to his ear, listening carefully to the faint scratchy voices.

He sniffed: nothing of current use, and not a whisper of the Princess Christina's Cerulean Star pendant. Good – the substitution had not been noticed, then. Fox-Torrington disassembled the device, dispersing and hiding the parts again.

He changed his clothes, swapping his gentleman's attire for the sedate middle-class working man's outfit. He slipped an envelope containing money into his jacket's inner pocket; he filled his coin purse with pennies. A touch of colour, applied with a toothbrush, darkened the hair of his temples and side-whiskers to their natural shade, and a bowler hat finished the ensemble.

He surveyed himself in the long mirror and tugged at his dull waistcoat. Acceptable. One button almost matched the others, and the jacket sleeves were a fraction too short. He nodded slowly. Really, Nell was brilliant with details. How might she feel about being recruited? Overall, the effect was convincing; he looked like a respectable under-clerk or such.

A discreet knock heralded his clever maid's arrival. He smiled as he turned away from the mirror.

"Tom?" She said.

He reached for his gloves, then remembered he'd left them in the other room. He shrugged. He did not need them: not with *her*.

"Come in, Nell."

She did so; he caught a glimpse of the dust-sheeted, disused bedroom behind her as she entered and closed the door softly. She put the hamper down on the floor. The homelike fragrance of freshly baked bread drifted from it.

"There's my good girl. Thanks." As he kissed her briefly on the lips, he inhaled the scents of warm girl and rosemary perfumed soap. The second kiss lasted longer.

"Oh, sir!" she fluttered, "You *are* wicked!" She laughed. Her chestnut coloured curls bobbed against her cheeks.

He grinned at her. "You don't want my kiss? You'd better give it back, then!" He stepped away, crossed his arms and smiled his challenge.

She stepped closer.

"I think so, indeed, sir." She suited her action to his words, returned his kiss and added her own.

They drifted apart.

Nellie picked up the hamper, opened the dressing room door for him and handed him his neatly darned gloves. He drew them on.

"All clear downstairs?" he asked.

"Yes. All quiet." He stepped from the dressing room, into the disused bedroom, slid the window sash up quietly and threw his leg over the window sill.

"You'll be careful?" Nell urged.

"When am I not?" He touched her cheek tenderly and bestowed a kiss on her brow.

As he stepped out onto the tiles of the roof, she handed him the hamper.

It was an easy climb, followed by a shallow drop, and then he was at street level. He walked a short distance to a busier street and thence to Piccadilly where he could hail a horse-drawn omnibus.

CHAPTER THREE

Tom ducked between a rickety cart and stationary hackney Hansom cab and whistled. The rumble of the approaching omnibus wheels on cobblestones slowed to a halt. The near-side horse took the opportunity to lift her tail. He dodged between other horse- or steam-drawn vehicles, grabbed the rail of the omnibus, and swung himself onto the small boarding platform. He handed the conductor his tuppence, climbed the curved staircase to the upper deck and dropped into the corner of the bench-seat.

The straw underfoot still smelt damp after yesterday's rain. Tom wrinkled his nose, wriggled in his seat and adjusted the food hamper on his lap.

As he travelled east the houses and public buildings became less grand. Marble facades gave way to stone, which gave way to dusty brick. The streets were narrower, and often unpaved. The passers-by and his fellow passengers were dressed more plainly now, being of the middling sort. Only the occasional top hat appeared amongst the bowlers and caps.

He stood up, squeezed between the other passengers, and alighted just east of Covent Garden. Crossing the street to avoid passing the workhouse on the corner, he strode south-east, following the chime of Saint Clement Danes' bells.

As he entered an old familiar lane his pace altered, his stride shortening. He had been holding the hamper freely, by its handles. Now he tucked it tightly under his arm. He felt his fingers clench of their own accord, in sympathy with his tightening stomach.

He paused at a road intersection, and let a cart trundle by. As he stepped from the curb, some toff in a silk hat sped past in a swaying carriage. The imperious gaze brushed over him for a moment, and then was gone. He briefly touched his bowler hat. He was not Lord Fox-Torrington now: he was Thomas Hutchings again. The fingers of his left hand ached in remembered pain. He flexed them.

The carriage continued on its riotous way, scattering pedestrians and horse drawn vehicles alike. Cold, dirty water flung up by the carriage's wheels deluged a small girl selling flowers. The water dripped from her threadbare hem. Her thin shoulders sagged. She blinked, too tired to even swear at her unmindful persecutor.

Tom stepped towards her.

"How much are your flowers, lass?" he asked.

The girl dropped her gaze. "They're all muddied, sir…"

"It doesn't matter,"

The girl eyed him doubtfully.

"Penny-ha'penny each, sir?"

He examined the posies, passing over the cornflowers and roses and selecting pinks and carnations. He chose from the best of them the single presentable posy and gave her sixpence. Her eyes went wide.

"But, sir–"

"I know." He folded her fingers over the coin. "Keep it."

A smile flickered over her lips "Thank you, sir."

He watched her scuttle away through the street's bustle, stretching and flexing his aching deformed fingers. He remembered…

He was eight years old, small for his age, but big enough to sweep street crossings to earn pennies. Most of the rich folk would give him something for the sake of saving their shoes from the muck of the streets.

A gentleman tucked his silver-topped cane under his arm and opened his purse to extract a coin for Tom's services; a five-pound note blew out, fluttering along the street. Tom scrambled to catch and return it.

Pain shot through his fingers. The toff had struck his fingers with his cane.

"Take my money, would you, you little gutter-rat?" Tom felt his earlobe grasped in ungentle fingers, and yelped. "I'll have you up before the magistrate, thief!"

'But, sir –!"

"Don't lie, boy!"

Tom squirmed, wrenched himself free and fled.

He ran, darting left into an alley between two rows of houses. Shouts, footsteps and the clack of a police rattle closed in on him. He ducked under a line of billowing frayed washing strung between two back fences. The footsteps rushed past. The unlocked gate to his left hung ajar, squeaking in the breeze. He shoved it as he ran past and left it swinging. He kept going.

The sharp smells of soap, steam, and clean linen met his nostrils. A Chinese laundry. He squeezed through a gap in the fence and found himself in a compact courtyard. He stole across the slippery cobblestones and skulked between the billowing linens. He held his breath and listened for pursuit.

His hunters had doubled back and were now in the lane.

Tom snatched garments off the lines, tugged them on and bundled his cap and jacket into a cloth and knotted it. He pulled on a calico bonnet and stuck his head through the gap in the fence.

No-one.

His heart raced. He wanted to run. But that would draw attention.

He took a deep breath and entered the lane again, turning right instead of left. He tugged his bonnet tight and dawdled. No one would suspect a girl in a frock, pinafore and bonnet taking 'her' time in a rare chance to dodge work. He reached a main street and sped toward the safety of home.

The peppery scent of the flowers brought Tom back to the present. He relaxed his aching fingers.

It had been many years ago. There had been no money for doctors. His fingers had never healed properly. Now he had his own carriage, his own silver-topped cane, and more than enough to eat. Now he had the money to see his family never went hungry.

He turned off the wide, cobbled lane, into a narrower one. Gravel crunched under his feet. The dusty house-fronts on his left-hand side were thrown into their own shadow, while the occasional top window on the eastern side of the street gleamed dully in the light of the westering sun. Tom crossed to the sunnier side of the lane.

If only he could persuade his mother to move, he would buy her a little house. Somewhere pleasant, far from the East End. His family would want for nothing. Lord Edward Fox-Torrington would see to it.

The paint on the front door of the house where his mother lived was faded, but the front doorstep was scrubbed to perfect whiteness. He wished she wouldn't bother: none of the other tenants did.

He let himself into the narrow hall, ignored the narrow carpet-less staircase leading to other lodgings, and wiped his boots on the sacking mat by his family's door. He opened it and called:

"Ma? It's me..."

"Tommy, lovey!" Ma called, "We're in the front room."

He stepped into the 'front room' – the bedroom being the other end of the room screened off by a curtain - and put his bundles on the floor. He popped a penny into the slot of the gas meter near the door and stacked a pile more near it.

After hanging his coat and hat on a hook, he turned to greet his mother and sister, both seated by the fire.

"Hello, Ma," he smiled.

He bounded across the room, and opened his arms. His mother, still dressed in black, discarded her sewing and rose to meet him. He hugged her. Over her head he smiled and nodded to his sister.

"I brought you both something," he said.

He retrieved the hamper and the posy of flowers he'd bought from the street girl.

A photograph of Tom's father stood propped up on the shelf that did duty as a mantelpiece. He had paid for it just before his Dad's funeral. Tom took one of the carnations from the bunch and tucked it into the black sash still draping the humble *memento mori*.

He presented the rest of the flowers to his mother. "For you, Ma."

"They're luverly! Thank you, Tom." She accepted the flowers, inhaled and smiled, although her eyes glistened.

"Hello, Lizzie." He kissed his sister on the head and tickled the baby in her arms. "Have you chosen a name for my nephew yet?"

"We thought, p'rhaps, Jacob Thomas." Lizzie replied.

He smiled and nodded. "That's good. Dad would have liked that."

"Hope so." Her smile wobbled. "And a letter come from our Jacob; will you read it to us?"

"Of course, but supper first."

He presented his mother with the hamper, and placed the envelope with his Ma's rent on the mantelshelf.

His mother put the frying pan onto the fire to heat. The baby had fallen asleep in his young mother's arms, so Lizzie rose and took him to the other side of the room to tuck him into the ancient family crib.

When she returned, she covered the table with a bright cloth. Tom spread the supper on it; fresh white bread, bacon, cake and apples. Soon the kettle whistled loudly enough to drown out the hissing and spitting of the cooking bacon. Ma filled the teapot, while Tom sliced the bread.

They ate, Tom refilling their plates as often as they wanted.

"How's your job, Tom?" his mother asked, accepting a piece of cake.

"Good. The guvnor paid me extra because I did so well, last time."

"Why won't you tell us where you work, Tommy? We're family."

"You're not family to the Toffs I work for. They keep their secrets, they do."

Tom chose the freshest and shiniest of the apples and pressed it into his sister's hand. She took a big crunchy bite from it; the juice splashed. Tom brushed the drops from Lizzie's face. "Mucky pup!" He laughed at her, as though they were still children.

"'Lizbeth, you're never eating that apple *raw*!" Ma looked horrified. Lizzie shrugged.

"I like 'em raw, Ma. It don't do me no harm."

Chuckling, Tom chose an apple, too. He cut himself a slice and popped it into his mouth. Ma shook her head, speechless.

The light outside was fading. Ma turned the gas lamp up, and Lizzie passed Tom her husband's letter.

"What does it say?" Ma asked.

Tom unfolded the letter and read it to them. The fire crackled as it burned lower…

Hemmy carefully turned over the thick page of the huge pteridology tome. The watercolours of the illustrated ferns glowed in the light from the tall windows of their Library. She glanced up from her desk as Eli entered.

"Happy birthday, Hemmy." He smiled. The corners of his eyes

crinkled as he held out a small gift-wrapped box.

She sprang from her armchair, kissed Eli's cheek, and accepted the present from his hand. "What is it?"

She tore the bright wrapping, not waiting for an answer. Inside the paper was a cardboard box embossed with the words *Lancaster and Sons, Opticians*. Her eyebrows crinkled in perplexity. Did Eli consider her in need of spectacles?

He watched her face. "Go ahead, Hemmy. Open it."

"Oooh!" she cooed.

Inside was a shining silver-coloured fob watch. She laid the box on the desk, lifted the watch from its protective nest of satin, and pressed its catch to open it.

It was no small clock face within. She blinked as half a dozen concentric rings telescoped outward of their own accord and clicked into place, with barely a sound. A miniature lens graced the centre of the roundel capping the smallest ring.

Hemmy's eyes widened. She looked at Eli.

"Whatever is it? It's not a photographic camera?" It fitted easily in her palm and weighed less than Elias's pocket watch. "But it's so small."

"That's exactly what it is." His grin widened.

Her smile mirrored his. She flung her arms around Eli.

"It's wonderful, Eli! Thank you," she said. "Will you pose for me?"

"Certainly,"

She turned the instrument over and opened the back.

A small ground glass screen was held in place with four tiny catches. She gently tugged on them. She frowned. They were stiff.

"Would you like the instructions, Hemmy?" asked Eli.

She raised an eyebrow. Instructions? When had she ever needed instructions for any mechanical device?

She ignored him, pulled up a chair, and unpacked an array of accoutrements from the bottom of the box. Perhaps a special tool was provided? She took her time, and examined the elegant chain for fastening the watch-camera to a bodice, the extra exposure-plate holders and the bottles of chemicals.

Eli proffered the supplied instruction pamphlet.

"You - I –." Hemmy blinked at him. "I beg your pardon?" Surely, he was teasing her?

His eyes crinkled at the edges. His lips quivered.

Hemmy jumped from her chair, thrust her hands on her hips and pulled herself up to her full height.

"Oh, Elias - You *wretch*." She scowled.

He plopped down onto the armchair opposite the desk and laughed.

Hemmy bit her lip to quash her smile. She flung herself toward him and gently batted him about the head and shoulders with the instruction pamphlet.

"Oh, Hemmy..." He chortled. "Your face! *Instructions*, indeed."

Her chin crumpled. Her lips twitched. Her smile broke through.

Eli caught her batting hands in one of his. "Oh, please, desist! I need to breathe."

She dropped the pamphlet on the desk and laughed as he pulled her down onto his lap and hugged her until their laughter eased.

"I confess, Sweet," He swallowed a final laugh. "I am a little disappointed at the fiddly design of that thing. And it seems you need to replace the photographic plate every time you expose an image."

"It is a fascinating idea, though." She picked the miniature camera up from the desk. "Suppose we replaced these clips?"

"Yes." He looked over her shoulder.

"Perhaps we could replace the little metal plates with impregnated celluloid?" said Hemmy.

"From your Box Brownie? Excellent idea."

She grinned, and gathered up the camera and accoutrements. "Let's!" She scampered into the hall, and down the stairs, towards Eli's former-

20

scullery dark room.

CHAPTER FOUR

T he hired carriage turned the corner into St. James's Square. Fox-Torrington pulled his purse from his pocket and pressed a wad of banknotes into Nell's hand.

"Now, Nellie, here's the money. You know what to do."

Nell nodded and placed the notes into her beaded purse.

"Remember, you're used to large sums," he said. "Show no surprise at the bids. This is your limit." He handed her a folded note.

She opened the piece of paper and read the amount, concealing all emotion.

"Perfect," he said.

The carriage halted outside the Auction house. Fox-Torrington looked out of the window. In front of them, one carriage dropped off a wealthy-looking couple then drove away. A gentleman paused before the marble-columned doors of the classically-styled building, apparently looking for somebody. When his acquaintance arrived, they shook hands then entered together.

Time to make their entrance. He shoved his purse back into his pocket.

"I'll have the coachman drive around the block, and I'll enter a few minutes after you: we don't know each other."

Nell clutched his hand. "Suppose someone outbids me?" she asked.

"Then we try another way."

He offered his hand to steady her as she stepped from the carriage. "Good luck, Lady Eleanor." He tipped his hat.

"Thank you, Lord Fox-Torrington." She nodded farewell. "Good afternoon."

Fox-Torrington re-entered the carriage, leaned back into the upholstered seat and banged on the roof with his cane. The carriage moved off.

A white-gloved attendant directed Elias through the door marked 'Private Auction.'

Light streamed through multi-paned windows and glimmered from ornate gasoliers. Paintings hung from the picture rail. Rows of seats faced the podium, and settees and couches were arranged against the walls, to leave room for the bidders to browse and examine.

A murmur of polite conversation came from the assembly. Glasses clinked as waiters moved among them, serving champagne. Elias accepted a glass and sat on a large, leather settee to leaf through the catalogue.

He pulled out his fountain pen, and noted several items he had previewed.

The auctioneer banged his gavel to start the proceedings. The crowd hushed and moved toward the podium, some taking seats, some remaining standing. The bidding began.

Elias sat back and observed the other competing bidders. A loud-spoken American quaffed his champagne and waved his numbered paddle for his bid. An elegantly dressed lady sat calmly on a Rococo divan. He recognised Fox-Torrington, who watched the proceedings with heavy, bored-looking eyes, rousing himself only rarely to bid.

"Sold for twenty guineas to–"

A familiar bass rumble muttered from the far side of the group; "Dash it all, I wanted that."

Elias covered his smile with his hand. Lord William Alford had been a friend of his family's since before Eli had been born. Alford caught his eye and nodded in his direction. Elias waved back in greeting.

"Is that a bid, Mr Barrington?" asked the auctioneer.

Elias' eyes widened. He blushed. Caught out; not concentrating. He glanced at the sale lot: a collection of fine hunting guns. He swallowed. Lordy, why would he bid for those? He didn't like guns. He'd rather fish.

He shook his head. "No, thank you. No bid." He lowered his paddle well out of the auctioneer's sight.

Lord Alford shook his head, laughed and raised the bid, staring down his competition.

"Thirty to finish the bid." Lord Alford's voice boomed across the room.

The gavel slammed onto the podium. "Sold!"

Elias puffed out his breath in relief. Lord Alford grinned and raised his glass to Elias.

Next was a Brussels carpet. Fox-Torrington won the bid. His smile was smug.

"Next we have Lot number one hundred and sixty-six," said the auctioneer.

Elias sat up. Here it was.

A deep, box-like frame, glassed in to protect the artefact it held from damage, was displayed.

"A vintage leather bridle with silver decorations and bit. This, ladies and gentleman, is purported to be a kelpie bridle. What do I hear for this legendary piece?"

The crowd murmured. A few heads shook. There were no bids.

Elias started the bidding. "Three pounds." It was low, but he might get away with it, since there was so little interest.

"Three pounds ten," shouted the American, as he snaffled another champagne glass from a passing waiter.

The Lady stood and raised her paddle. "Four."

Elias raised his hand. *Four ten.*

The American shook his paddle at the auctioneer. *Five.*

Elias' heart raced. He hadn't expected a fight.

"Five and ten shillings." The woman stepped toward the podium, her eyes bright.

"Six." Elias slipped the catalogue into his coat pocket.

The woman glared in Elias's direction. "Eight pounds."

Damn. Elias grabbed a drink from the waiter's tray.

The American shook his head, downed his drink and shrugged. The woman smiled sweetly.

"Going once." The auctioneer looked at Elias.

Elias's heart skipped a beat. Eight pounds. For a scruffy bridle, which may not even be what I think it is. One might buy a horse for less in the Antipodean colonies. What would Hemmy say? Perhaps he needn't tell her.

"Ten to finish the bid." Elias rose from the settee and raised his paddle firmly.

The woman frowned, shrugged, and shook her head. Elias placed his untouched glass on the tray with an unsteady hand.

The thud of the gavel filled the room.

"Sold, to Mr. Barrington. Thank you, sir. The next Lot…"

Tom sat at the dressing table and adjusted the mirror to make the most of the light. He inhaled the familiar, earthy scent of greasepaint and sighed, feeling the tension in his brows and shoulders release. He missed this old routine, and the careful layering of face paint, of costume, the process of creating a new persona. He took care, blended his colours thoroughly, and kept his lines fine, so the makeup looked natural and realistic. His artifice must not be detected.

He opened a small bottle. The sharp smell of the spirit gum penetrated his nostrils. He held fine crepe hair fibres in the steam from the kettle, and watched the kinks relax until they matched the wave of his natural whiskers. He tipped a small brush with gum, layered the hairs and trimmed them to shape.

Tom looked at himself in the small mirror. A fine full beard. He examined the lines crinkled at the corners of his eyes. Convincing. His cheeks looked suitably saggy. His skin had taken on the faded look of age; in reality, the result of an arsenic wafer he had ingested earlier.

He picked up the wafer tin: *Dr. Mackenzie's improved harmless arsenic wafers will produce the most lovely complexion the imagination could desire.* His lip twitched at the irony of the advertisement's claim.

He discarded the cloth tucked into his collar, reached for the jacket hanging on the mirrored wardrobe behind him and slipped it on. The old-fashioned suit fit perfectly. He grinned; he looked quite the distinguished, elderly gentleman. His own Ma would be hard pressed to recognise him.

He selected a hat, picked up a worn cane to complete the ensemble, then crept down the servants' narrow stairs, past the door to the servants' hall and the kitchens. Would he hear Nell's voice? Or was she still upstairs, clearing the table after luncheon?

He eased open the door at street level, scanned the empty alley, smiled and closed the door behind him.

The Drawing room door opened. Hemmy closed her book and placed it on the octagonal side table by the settee.

"A gentleman to see you, sir." Hannah stood in the doorway, a small silver tray in her hand. At Elias's nod she entered and presented the visiting card it held.

Eli perused the card.

"Smith? I don't remember. Oh, yes. He did write." He sighed and put down his pen. "I wonder what he wants? I wish we need not bother; I want to finish this report."

"Perhaps he won't stay long," suggested Hemmy.

He indicated Hannah should show the visitor up. Hemmy stood, straightened her skirts and patted her hair. Their guest entered, and removed his hat.

"Mr Barrington?" The elderly, bearded man shook Elias's hand politely, but Hemmy noticed he remained gloved. Odd. Perhaps he suffers from arthritis?

"Smith is my name."

Eli nodded in greeting. "This is my wife, Mrs Barrington."

"How do you do, madam," He bowed in Hemmy's direction.

"How do you do, Mr Smith." Hemmy nodded and smiled. "Please, take a seat?"

"Ah. Yes, thank you." He remained motionless until Hemmy lowered herself into a chair. He took a seat opposite Elias.

"It's very good of you to see me, Mr Barrington," said Smith. "I've heard great things about your research." He glanced at the book on the side table. The author's name was easily visible: E.J. Barrington.

"That is good of you to say. What can I do for you, Mr Smith?" asked Eli.

"I approach you on behalf of my employer, Mr Mills." He squeezed the hat rim. "He would like to make you a business proposal."

"Indeed?" Eli glanced at Hemmy, dabbed his eye.

What? Hemmy lifted inquisitive eyebrows.

Eli tugged his ear lobe.

Hemmy's eyes widened. Oh, yes. Their signal. Elias's idea. Most men disliked talking business or science with a woman, but Eli was not most men. Meanwhile, she would play the role of Angel in the House for appearances' sake. It was Expected.

"If you would excuse me, I will leave you gentlemen to talk." She rose from her chair.

The men stood.

"Of course, my dear," said Eli. "As you wish." With the eye away from Smith, he winked at her.

"Cigar, Mr Smith?" said Eli. "Or would you prefer brandy?"

Crystal glass clinked as Hemmy closed the door behind her. She smiled. Eli was stalling for time until she could reach the Library.

Hemmy hastened down the hall and slipped into the Library. Once there, she pulled the velvet curtains closed, and pressed one of the panels in the wall nearest the Drawing room. It opened to reveal a secret cupboard-sized compartment.

Two objects rested on a shelf in the concealed cubbyhole: a stubby, cylindrical device constructed from brass, and a binaural stethoscope with ivory ear pieces.

She drew the ends of the cylinder apart and extended it into a foot-long periscope. She positioned the top hole over a peephole above her head and rested her eye against the bottom eyepiece. Her field of view was small but quite clear.

Mr Smith sat with his back to her. Eli sat opposite. He looked once in her direction then continued his conversation. Hemmy applied the earpieces and pressed the stethoscope bell against the wall.

"Now, sir, tell me about this proposition." Eli's voice was distinct.

"Mr Barrington, your scientific reputation precedes you." Mr Smith nestled his hat on his lap. "Mr Mills has learned that you plan to conduct an expedition to search for the water kelpie in the Scottish Highlands."

Hemmy's heart skipped a beat. He was going away again. Her heart sank. But it was so soon. He had only just come back.

Eli's eyebrows lifted. He glanced up toward the peephole and shifted in his chair.

"He would like to be involved," continued Mr Smith. Eli looked back at him.

"In what capacity, Mr Smith?"

"We hope you could help us capture at least one breeding pair."

Eli frowned, but did not interrupt, so Smith continued.

"With such powerful beasts to drive machinery in place of steam engines, England need never be dependent on expensive, filthy coal again." He leaned forward. "The British Empire will lead the world into the new Century. Mr Mills proposes to pay for the entire expedition, provided you allow his representative to accompany you."

Eli's back stiffened and he straightened his shoulders.

"I have no need of financial support, Mr Smith. I am able to pay for my own expeditions."

Hemmy shook her head; Eli was just like her father. Papa, too, had baulked at being paid, like a common artisan, for his scientific research, for practicing his passion.

Smith spoke: "Perhaps a fully equipped laboratory would be of interest to you? And full credit on any papers presented to the Royal Society and the Cryptozoological Society?"

Elias shook his head. "I already have two excellent laboratories in the attic."

Smith lifted his head toward the ceiling. His eyes returned to Elias as he continued:

"Also, it is not my intention to capture these cryptic animals, merely to scientifically prove their existence to the satisfaction of the Royal Society and the Cryptozoological Society."

"But, sir," Smith's voice was calm and entreating. "If we could breed these mighty creatures! Surely you can see the benefits? Cheap, clean energy in abundance! It would revolutionise manufacturing."

"No doubt," Eli crossed his arms and shook his head. "But expeditions of this kind are dangerous."

Hemmy shivered. Eli had nearly lost his life on more than one occasion. Her fingers prickled. As she reached for Eli's letter in her pocket, the periscope knocked against the wood panelling. She winced. Had they heard her? She peered through the eyepiece.

"I'm sorry, but I cannot help Mr Mills." Eli shook his head. "I am not prepared to place anyone at risk."

"Mr Mills will be greatly disappointed."

And so is Mr Smith, Hemmy sniffed. The fingers of his left hand were clenched.

Elias stood and rang for the footman.

"Unfortunately, I do not suit his needs," he said, "but thank him for the offer, Mr. Smith. And thank you for your time."

"I'll see myself out." Smith plopped his hat on his head.

Hemmy heard two sets of footsteps cross the room. She shoved the periscope back into the cupboard and stuffed the stethoscope into the pocket under her overskirt, next to Eli's letter. She hurried from the Library to meet them in the hallway. She smiled sweetly, as she accompanied their guest downstairs to the front door.

"Please convey my regrets to Mr Mills, and thank him for considering me for his partnership." Elias offered his hand to their visitor.

Mr Smith seemed to barely notice Elias's polite remarks. Instead he scanned the hall, like a man who had lost something. His gaze lingered on the lock as the footman opened the door for him.

He paused in the doorway, shook Elias's hand absent-mindedly, opened his mouth as if to say something, then seemed to think better of it. He tipped his hat in Hemmy's direction and departed.

They returned to the Drawing room.

Elias sank onto the settee. "Well, what did you think of that?" he asked.

"I think Mr Smith did not expect you to refuse the offer." She sat down next to him. "He seemed frustrated that you did not share his enthusiasm for the project."

"He did."

"You're leaving again?" she asked calmly.

"Ah, yes." He hesitated, "Apparently."

"And you were going to tell me about that, when?" she asked, frowning. "How is it a stranger knows of your plans before your own wife?"

Eli shook his head. He looked baffled. "Well, I didn't know for sure, myself, before the auction."

Hemmy drew in a deep breath. "What auction is that, Elias?" She crossed her arms.

"I told you; the one where I bought the kelpie's bridle."

"No,"

"Mills must have attended the auction. That's how he knew - or guessed – about the expedition."

Hemmy slumped backwards into her seat, ran her fingers through her hair and groaned. Sometimes Eli was the most frustrating of men. Brilliant, but disorganised, unpunctual, and obsessed with detail, when at work. Aarggh!

"Hemmy, what's wrong?"

"You have told me almost *nothing* of any of this." She blinked rapidly, feeling her eyes fill.

Eli looked at her, wide eyed. "I'm sure I did."

Hemmy shook her head. Eli looked stricken. "I'm so sorry. Ask about anything."

Hemmy frowned. If she was going on this expedition – and she was, since Eli should not even be let out of the house alone - what was she getting herself into? Smith had mentioned a 'kelpie.'

"What on earth is a 'kelpie'?" she asked.

"A species of *each uisce*."

Hemmy shook her head.

"A Waterhorse," said Eli. "It lives in rivers or lochs and has the strength of ten horses."

"Hmmm…" An advantage to Mr Mills, indeed. "Mr Smith seemed interested in their strength as well." She rubbed her chin. "The new steam technology is fine for the rich, like us, but it benefits the poor very little."

"Agreed," said Eli. "But would the poor derive any benefit from the kelpie-based technology?"

"The farm labourers who are still jobless, the factory workers who run the steam machines?" She shook her head. "No: I would foresee only lowered costs and increased profits for the factory owners."

He took her hand in his. "I won't condone enslaving living creatures for needless profit."

She nodded. Ever the idealist. That's why she loved him. She squeezed his hand.

"So, Eli, why did he ask *you* to find this creature?"

"Most scientists believe it's just a legend."

"And it isn't?"

"I think it exists. And now I have the bridle, I intend to find it."

"Why does a kelpie need a bridle?" she asked, "and why do *you* need one?"

"Legend says that he, who holds the bridle, controls the kelpie." Eli enfolded Hemmy's hand in his and kissed it gently. "I'm going to use the bridle to catch one."

"Only if you take me with you," whispered Hemmy.

CHAPTER FIVE

Pale sunlight shone through the newly-installed skylight of the Barrington's attic laboratory, creating a golden patchwork on the wooden floor. Larger squares of light illuminated the floor in front of the un-curtained windows. It spilled over the watercolours of Hemmy's fern collection stacked on one end of her desk, illuminated her notes and glinted off the ornate brass microscope Papa had given to her last year for her twenty-first birthday. A child's picture of a vibrant red bottlebrush tree was framed and held the place of honour above her desk.

She turned the page of her current research book and rolled her shoulders. She looked up and around the room to rest her eyes.

Eli worked beside her. In contrast to her ordered, uncluttered desk, his desk was covered in books, journals and sketches of cryptids from previous expeditions.

He leaned forward to check the maps of more recent kelpie sightings that were pinned to the wall above his desk. The yellowed McGregor of Lochan Slochd report was fastened under them. Experiments in progress, and inventions both incomplete and finished, crowded the other work tables.

There was a knock on the laboratory door.

"Come in," said Elias. Hemmy shut her book and turned to face towards the door as it opened.

"Excuse me, sir, madam, but there's a package here for you, sir," said Hannah.

Hemmy's eyes brightened. "Something new?" she asked Eli.

"Patience, dearest." He smiled and cleared a section of workbench.

The footman brought it in, laid the large, flat package on the bench top as instructed, and then withdrew.

Hemmy edged closer as Elias removed the string and outer wrappings from it. He lifted a deep frame, or shallow case, from the box. Hemmy stepped closer to see.

"Whatever is it?" she eyed it. "Art?"

"No, indeed!" he chuckled, tapping a small hand-written card in the lower corner.

"This, my dearest Hemmy, is my find from the auction: the reputed Kelpie's Bridle."

Hemmy examined the artefact. It appeared to be formed from long strips of fragmented, shiny, silvery cloth. Or perhaps it was leather? It was embedded in something to preserve it. She squinted. Wax, perhaps. She frowned; it was hard to tell under the glass in the frame. A few crumbling, tarnished pieces of metal, once bright, had presumably held the pieces of harness together long ago.

"I would like your professional opinion on this object," said Eli.

He flipped the frame over, picked up a small tool from the bench and began to prise up the tacks holding the backing board in. He lifted it out, followed by the mounting, and placed it face up before Hemmy.

She retrieved a magnifying glass from her desk drawer and examined one edge of the bridle. Particles of it had crumbled free of the rest. She picked up a needle probe.

"May I?" she asked.

Eli nodded.

She lifted a few of the specks out of the surrounding wax, deposited them on a microscope slide and covered them with a delicate round glass coverslip.

Taking the slide to the microscope on her desk, she slid it under the Objective lens and focussed.

"It's not fabric: there's no weave. And it's organic, not manufactured. I can't see square cell walls. I believe this is animal tissue." She changed the magnification and looked again, examining the texture. "Equine epidermis?" she frowned, pondering. "Yes, quite possibly genuine. And if it is?"

"According to my folklore research it's used to both summon and control a kelpie."

"And can it stop it shapeshifting between kelpie, horse, and human form?"

Eli eyes widened and he raised an eyebrow. He glanced at the book of folklore on her desk.

"You've been researching."

"Of course." Hemmy nodded. "But Eli..." Her smile slipped. She had read enough stories to know the risks; magical creatures were tricky. "Doesn't Folklore also warn how dangerous it is to attempt to place an Uncanny creature under subjugation?"

Elias rubbed his nose and examined the card in the frame. He appeared not to have heard her question.

Fox-Torrington donned his top hat, stepped from the tranquillity of his favourite barber's shop, with its soft click of scissors, civilised conversation and calming scents of shaving soap and hair tonic, and emerged into the cacophony and stink of the city street. The smells of stale beer, food, smoke and stray dogs trespassed on his nostrils. Hooves clattered on the cobblestones, kicking up clouds of dust and dried dung.

The brisk warm wind swept them away.

Voices shouted. Street vendors touted their wares. A gentleman hurried along the street towards him, head down, one hand holding onto his hat. He collided with Fox-Torrington, murmured an apology, tipped his hat, and scurried on.

Fox-Torrington felt for his wallet and watch. Both were still there. He let out his breath; his pocket hadn't been picked. He paused and checked his other pockets. In one he found a piece of paper, folded. He opened it.

10 30, 13 08 94 54B Eaton. - The Curator.

He snorted. No surprise, but irritating, nonetheless. Still, the Curator had to do something with his time. Fox-Torrington stepped into the lee of a building, away from the wind and from prying eyes. He flicked open his vesta case and extracted a match. Its flame charred the edge of the paper. The note disintegrated as it fluttered to the ground. He smiled, trod the black flakes underfoot and strode off.

The waiting room had been furnished in the latest style: flocked silk wallpaper, a small Axminster carpet in front of the plain but sturdy desk. A small light blinked on top of the desk. It was Amberonically powered. Impressive. As it was meant to be; Fox-Torrington kept his eyebrows still.

The dull, grey lackey behind the desk straightened his back. He nodded to Fox-Torrington.

"You may go in," he said.

Fox-Torrington checked his watch unhurriedly, then put it away. He eyed the man as if he'd not heard him clearly.

"The Curator will see you now," he repeated, as he opened the office door. Fox-Torrington hid his smile, took his time rising, and entered.

The Curator's office had been furnished as a study; a large oak desk faced the doorway, a cheery fire crackled in the grate behind it. The Curator sat behind the desk; a faceless shape outlined against the light. A nice trick, if not very original. Fox-Torrington smiled and paused in the doorway. It didn't hurt to make his presence felt.

"Ah, Collector." The Curator looked up from his paperwork. "Come in. Take a seat."

So, I rate a chair, do I? I should think so, too.

"Thank you, sir," Fox-Torrington said.

There was no seat set before the desk. A hard, upright chair stood against the wall. Fox-Torrington shifted it forward and arranged it in front of the Curator.

The Curator opened a large ledger and ran the tip of his pen down the page.

"This is very impressive." He leaned back in his upholstered chair. The firelight shone on his meticulously manicured fingernails as he steepled his fingers. "Yes. We are pleased."

Leaning forward again, he opened a cash box, withdrew several large denomination banknotes, placed them in an envelope and laid it on the desk.

"And how are you progressing with Mr. Mills' kelpie's bridle?" he asked.

Fox-Torrington slid the envelope off the desk, slipped it into his coat pocket, resumed his seat and mirrored the Curator's posture.

"I have located it, Curator. I shall have it in my possession within the next forty-eight hours."

CHAPTER SIX

Pipe smoke and the scent of beer drifted through the air. An untrained but tuneful baritone, who'd had more than a drop in, favoured the assembly with his rendition of a popular hymn. Charles chuckled. Those were not the words he'd heard in church.

Gas lights reflected from the glasses, from metal, polished wood and mirrors.

Charles leaned back into the padded bench in his favourite corner of the pub as Rogers approached. A barmaid wove her way between the patrons towards him. He moved his new brown bowler hat with the black band out of harm's way as, smiling, she slid two beers onto the table.

"There you are, dearie," she said.

Charles nodded and smiled back. "Ta, luv."

He sighed. It made a nice change to be served, instead of serving drinks himself.

Rogers tucked his gloves inside his coachman's hat and sat opposite Charles. Charles pushed one beer towards him.

"Thanks, mate." Rogers took his first sip, and sighed, his expression blissful.

"How are things going?" asked Charles, "Anything interesting?"

"He's studying birds this week," replied Rogers.

"Birds?" The lines between Charles's eyebrows deepened. How would that interest Fox-Torrington and the Collector Network?

"Aye." Rogers leaned closer. "He's making little models, like. He's paying my lad Harry to measure how far they fly across the park and then take them back up to him in the attic."

"Righto. Thanks." Charles lifted his glass. "Cheers."

The windows of Lady Emily Carmody's mansion blazed with lights. A bright moon, just past full, shone on the carriages that drew up to the doors, dropped off their passengers, and departed down the drive.

Liveried footmen opened the doors for guests resplendent in silk top hats or light evening cloaks. Hermia and Elias wove their way through the crowd in the entrance hall, surrounded by the murmur of polite conversations. The scents of roses and ladies' perfume enveloped them. Bright, starched, white shirt-fronts and glittering jewels shone under the gas chandeliers and were reflected in many gold-framed mirrors.

In the ladies' cloak room Hemmy slipped off her evening cloak and left it in the care of the maid. Hemmy examined herself in the long mirror Lady Carmody had thoughtfully provided, and puffed up her leg o' mutton sleeves. Her silk gown was turquoise blue, Elias's favourite colour on her. A net of aquamarines caressed her shoulders and snuggled on her décolletage. More jewels flashed amongst the gold of her upswept curls. She smiled, picked up her fan, checked that her dance card hung from her wrist, and left the cloakroom.

She returned to the hall, and searched the crowd for Eli. Her heart throbbed; there he was, outside the ballroom door, waiting for her. She made her way through a flock of white-gowned debutantes.

His face lit up as she drew near, and she blushed. He took her outstretched hand and kissed her fingers, gave her his arm and escorted her into the ballroom.

The quartet had almost finished tuning up. The pianist played a note for the violinist. One discordant note slid into harmony as the musician sharpened one string by a tone.

Small knots of people chatted. As Hemmy passed one group, a quiet musical laugh and several masculine chuckles rose above the cheerful murmur. A tall, immaculately-dressed, dark-haired man, whose ruby cuff links glinted with each gesture, held his audience captivated.

Hemmy covered her mouth with her fan. "Who's he?" She whispered in Eli's ear. "He certainly seems popular."

Eli's gaze followed Hemmy's. He winced. "Lord Edward Fox-Torrington," he murmured. "Ah, there's Sir Lachlan and Lady Lucy. Shall we say good evening?"

He steered Hemmy in the opposite direction, towards the couple standing near the unlit fireplace filled with an arrangement of summer flowers. Hemmy acknowledged several other friends and acquaintances as they made their way across the ballroom. Sir Lachlan and his wife greeted them cordially, and the gentlemen found seats for the ladies until the dancing started.

A familiar face approached Hemmy; her friend, Mary. Her copy followed half a step behind, in the shape of her twin sister, Sarah. Eli stood up as the young ladies drew near.

"Good evening, Hermia," said Mary. Her calm grey eyes were brightened by her smile.

"Dear Mary," Hemmy kissed Mary on the cheek and embraced Sarah. "Good evening, Sarah." Hemmy turned to Eli. "Elias, do you remember my friends, Miss Sinclair and Miss Sarah Sinclair?"

"Of course," Elias bowed. "I'm delighted to see you again, ladies. I hope you are both well?" he replied.

"Thank you, yes," said Sarah and Mary nodded agreement, and their chestnut curls bounced. "We are both well," they said in unison.

From nearby, the glitter of star-like jewels in a cloud of white hair distracted Hemmy's attention, as Lady Carmody glided through the room and greeted her guests.

Lady Carmody caught Hemmy's gaze, nodded and smiled at her. She made her way towards their small group.

"Look," whispered Sarah to her sister.

"Lady Carmody's coming this way," said Mary.

"She's wearing a bustle," whispered Sarah. "Are they back in fashion?" She tugged at her skirts and frowned. "I shall have to make an appointment with our tailor in the morning."

"No need," Hemmy whispered, "It's just her ladyship's quirk." Hemmy sighed; she wished she had the courage to wear what suited her, regardless of fashion. The statuesque Lady Emily always looked so elegant.

The twins curtsied as their hostess arrived and wished them a good evening.

"Good evening, Miss Sinclair, and Miss Sinclair." Lady Carmody smiled a greeting.

"Hermia, my dear, how good of you to come!" Her Ladyship offered her cheek for Hermia's kiss and gave Elias her hand. "I expected you to be in the country by now."

"We would be, Aunt," said Hermia, "but Elias has some things he wishes to complete here in town first."

Her Aunt Emily lowered her voice. "And by 'things' you mean he's tinkering with those extraordinary devices, with my little brother?" She chuckled and glanced at Elias, who was politely conversing with Mary and Sarah. "Or that he's leaving you behind again, to go off gallivanting all over the world chasing Untamed Galliformes?"

Hemmy shrugged gracefully, and a wry smile flickered over her lips. "Both, actually."

Lady Carmody squeezed Hemmy's hand, sighed and shook her head.

The band struck up, playing a lively quadrille. Hemmy's toe tapped to the beat. The twins' partners arrived and whisked them away.

"Excuse me, I must find Lord Carmody." Lady Carmody excused herself.

As Lady Carmody moved away Hemmy noticed the tall man with the rubies. He sauntered across the room, surprisingly light on his large feet. He was heading in their direction, to speak to a friend or acquaintance, she presumed. Probably one of the knot of gentlemen standing near the fireplace.

Hemmy raised an eyebrow: had he just surreptitiously checked his appearance in the over-mantel mirror? How ill-bred. And he was coming this way…

"Good evening, Barrington," he extended his hand to Elias.

"Torrington. Good evening." Eli shook the man's hand briefly.

"I wonder if I might trouble you for an introduction to your lovely wife?"

"Of course." Eli wrapped his arm around hers. "Hermia, may I present Lord Edward Fox-Torrington? Torrington, Mrs Barrington."

As Lord Fox-Torrington stepped towards her, the faint scents of costly ylang-ylang, bergamot, and orange hair oil wafted over her. His fingers encircled Hermia's hand. He bowed and kissed her fingers. The gesture was perfectly proper, but Hermia felt that she was being deliberately charmed. He was certainly over-confident. This was a man not accustomed to being refused.

"Enchanted," Fox-Torrington said. "May I have the honour of this dance, Mrs. Barrington?"

Hemmy checked her dance card, relieved the first dance was spoken for - by her husband.

"I'm sorry, but this dance is already taken." With a polite smile, she examined the remaining dances. Her list was already quite full. She found a blank place, later in the evening. He would have to be content with that. "Do you know the *Sir Roger De Coverley*?" she asked.

Fox-Torrington's eyebrow lifted slightly. "I do."

"The 'Sir Roger' it is, then." She wrote his name into her programme, closed her card and placed it in her bag.

"I look forward to it." Lord Fox-Torrington smiled, and retired.

"Is he a good friend of yours?" she asked Eli, as Fox-Torrington retreated into the crowd.

"An acquaintance, from my Club," he replied. "Why? Is something wrong?"

"No, nothing," she smiled. There was nothing wrong; only something not quite *right*. She dismissed the feeling and gave Eli her hand for him to lead her onto the dance floor.

Hermia saw Fox-Torrington occasionally during the night, always surrounded by feminine attendees with fluttering fans and eyelashes. As the evening wore on, she then lost sight of him among the twirling dancers.

Her heart raced and her cheeks were pink after she had danced a polka, so she and her partner paused for champagne and ices, then returned to the dance floor. The Misses Sinclair and their partners, with Hemmy and Eli, made up three of the pairs in a graceful Lancers Quadrille which allowed Hemmy to regain her breath. Later, Eli waltzed past with Lady Carmody and winked at Hemmy.

Just before supper, her promised dance partner joined her. The clock chimed a quarter to twelve as the Colonel bowed.

"Mrs Barrington, I'm sorry, but I must ask you to excuse me." He frowned. "I regret I must break my engagement for this dance."

"I hope there is nothing wrong, Colonel?"

"My wife is indisposed and I must return her home. The megrim, you know. I hope you will forgive me."

"Of course. I'm so sorry." She laid her hand briefly on his sleeve. "I understand. Please, convey my best wishes to your wife for a quick recovery."

"I will. Thank you. Good evening." He bowed over her hand, and retreated towards the exit.

Hemmy perused the crowd. Perhaps there was someone of her acquaintance with whom she could chat and while away the time until the next dance began?

She spotted Eli across the room, tending to the Colonel's afflicted wife. He nodded to the Colonel as he arrived and spirited his wife away. He was now as partnerless as Hemmy.

He caught her eye and smiled. Hemmy's heart fluttered as she watched him cross the floor. His dress suit fitted perfectly. Well, *almost* perfectly; it was a trifle snug across the breadth of his shoulders. All his adventurous outdoor activity must be keeping him fit. Or his tailor was losing his touch… His eyes twinkled as he bowed formally to her.

"May I have this dance?" he asked.

Hemmy glanced quickly around the ballroom. An extra dance with her husband was not *quite* good etiquette, but perhaps no-one would notice, or even mind, since it was the last ball of the Season? She smiled and nodded, and felt a little wicked as he led her across the floor.

She loved to dance, especially with Eli. He was an accomplished dancer and she found his combination of strength and gentleness appealing. As she placed her hand on his shoulder and caressed the muscles of his upper arm through the rich fabric of his tailcoat, he smiled. Hemmy raised her eyebrow. Perhaps the fit of his jacket was neither co-incidental nor accidental? Perhaps he had ordered it made that way? The Natural Scientists had a term for it: *courtship display*. For her?

Her eyes met his and he gazed warmly down at her. She blushed.

"I'll miss this when I'm away," he whispered.

She swallowed, her throat now tight. Those dashed expeditions! Her smile faded.

"What is it?" he asked her.

"Just as well I'm coming on this trip to Scotland with you, then," replied Hemmy with her most confident smile.

"No, love. It's too dangerous," he whispered in her ear as he leaned close. She felt his warm breath on her skin.

Hemmy frowned. She tilted her head away. Why was it too dangerous for her, if it was not too dangerous for him? She tightened her grip on his shoulder. If he went, it would not be alone. Somehow, she would change his mind.

The music finished, and the current groups of dancers drifted apart. The quartet turned the pages of their sheet music to the next tune.

"Now, Mrs Barrington, may I take you in to supper?" Eli asked.

She gave him her hand. A strategic withdrawal was called for, while she thought of another plan. Meanwhile, perhaps a morsel of something, and a cup of tea… or a cup of champagne punch?

"You may, Mr Barrington." She smiled up at him, "I would be delighted to take supper with you."

Fox-Torrington murmured a polite excuse to the gaggle of ladies flocking around him. He smiled, bowed and retired from the ballroom in the direction of the Gentleman's Hat room.

Once out of sight of the general crowd, he changed course towards the supper room, then diverted again and slipped out through the Conservatory into the garden.

After the warmth, the perfumed bodies, and the candlelight of the ballroom, the night air cooled his face as he glided from shadow to shadow. Dew-drenched grass and garden borders soaked his silk-clad feet and shoes to the ankles.

The garden wall loomed ahead like a black cliff. The polished tips of its decorative metal spikes reflected the streetlamps beyond. He hauled himself up, manoeuvred around the spikes and dropped down onto the footpath on the other side.

An unmarked hired carriage waited for him a few yards away. He got in, pulled down the blinds and banged on the roof with his silver-topped cane. The carriage rattled off along the cobblestones.

He tugged off his wet shoes and socks and untied his white bow tie. His formal jacket and waistcoat followed, replaced by warm, dark-coloured clothing, socks and soft soled footwear. He pulled on a woollen Coachman's greatcoat to complete the ensemble, then slipped a satchel over one shoulder.

He peeped under the blinds. The carriage was passing through Mayfair, towards the Palace and beyond, to fashionable Belgravia and Knightsbridge. He steadied himself as the coach turned a corner. It slowed and pulled up on the western edge of Ennismore Gardens. He checked his pockets; he had everything. He telescoped his cane down to half its length, and slid it into the concealed pocket running from his hip to his knee. He smiled, donned a bowler hat, then alighted and strolled casually around the edges of the garden Square.

He turned right twice and paused by the locked park gate, opposite the Barrington's house. The moon was bright, but still low, and threw behind him the shadows of the park railings and the trees. The tall shadow of the row of townhouses reached out to join them. He looked up, but couldn't see the roofs from this angle.

The small upper floor windows were in darkness: the servants would still be working downstairs. The windows were larger and more ornamented the closer they were to street level. None were lit. Light from the entrance hall fell through the glass leadlights surrounding the front door, turning the white columns and porch a warm gold. A dimmer light shone up through the Area railings from the windows of the basement kitchen and servants' Dining room. Just as he had anticipated, the coast was clear.

Slow, steady footsteps echoed at the end of the street. He looked towards them. The silhouette of a Copper drew nearer. The badge on his helmet glinted as he passed under the streetlamp.

Fox-Torrington pulled out tobacco and a pipe from his coat pocket.

He stepped into the lea of an overhanging tree and lit his pipe. The tobacco caught and glowed. He leaned against the garden wall.

"Good evening, sir," said the Copper. "Taking the air?"

"Good evening, Constable," Fox-Torrington took another draw at his pipe, exhaled and sighed. He flourished the pipe. "You won't tell the missus, Officer?"

"You can rely on my discretion, sir." The Copper smiled.

"Cheers."

The Copper touched his helmet in a half salute, and trod away eastward.

Fox-Torrington finished the pipe, knocked the tobacco out on the park wall railing, and sauntered across the road toward the archway leading to the Mews behind the houses.

Stable smells met his nose as he walked down the lane between the two rows of coach houses. An upstairs light went out as he passed beneath it. That was one coachman who doesn't have to wait up to bring his master home in the small hours.

The Barrington's place was halfway along. Reaching it, he studied the outbuildings, with their freshly painted double carriage doors, and the guttering and drainpipes in good repair. That augured well, if the house was as well maintained. He stuffed the bowler hat, along with the coachman's greatcoat, behind a rain barrel.

One hand on a windowsill, the other on the drainpipe, and he was up, on the coach house roof. He extracted his cane from its hidden pocket

50

and padded along its ridgepole, using his cane for balance.

A narrow yard formed a gap between the out-buildings and the back of the house. He readjusted his satchel, for balance, as he studied potential routes. It was too far to jump, but he might walk the top of the dividing wall between this house and the next.

Done. Easy.

He grinned and rested for a moment on the roof of the servants' privy as he planned his next ascent. Up over the coal shed and scullery, first. Two windows, on the second floor, sported bars. Former nurseries, probably; the bars looked sturdy. Excellent. They could get him higher, nearer to attic level. He slipped his cane back into its hidden sheath and grabbed a drainpipe, his toes feeling for grip on the brick walls.

He gripped the window bars and hauled himself up, scrabbling to get his feet onto their lower edge. He climbed up, and balanced on the top rail. He could just reach the next window. It belonged to the servants' attic quarters. The window sill was deep in birds' nests debris and dead leaves that crackled under his fingers. Unused for years. He ran his gloved finger around the edge of the window frame. Probably nailed shut, too.

He scowled and peered through the dusty glass. This attic was not servants' quarters; it had been converted into Barrington's laboratory. Moonlight spreading across the floor, suggested there was one more possibility.

Someone might trouble themselves to nail shut a servants' disused window, but he doubted they would think to secure a skylight. A decorative course of projecting brick work provided him with toeholds. He boosted himself upwards and climbed onto the house roof.

Ha! His hunch had played true: there *was* a skylight.

He skirted the solid-looking chimneys, padded across to the skylight, and peered through the small panes of glass down into the dim attic. He tested the latch. It was locked. Oh, well, worth a try.

He flipped open the top of his cane to access a diamond-tipped cutting tool and scored the glass. He pulled protective goggles from one of several pockets and slipped them on, then tapped the score lines with a small mallet. The glass cracked and tinkled onto the floor below.

Reaching his hand through the gap, he released the latch and lifted the casement. He secured his rope around the chimneys and then around himself, wriggled through the window, and dropped silently to the floor. He unwound the rope, slipped his goggles onto his forehead and surveyed the moonlit attic.

A cluttered desk, loaded tables. Almost half the workspace was filled by a looming silver skeleton, somewhat birdlike. In one corner the iron filigree of a large square cage cast intricate shadows on the floor. Pistons and chains surmounted it, some chains descending through the floor. Some sort of goods conveyer, perhaps?

The desk was cluttered with notebooks, drawings, maps; the tables were covered with models and tools. He unscrewed another segment of his cane and shook a vial out onto his hand. There were two coloured liquids within, one pale blue and one slightly amber, separated by a fine membrane of glass. He tapped the ampoule; the membrane cracked. The two chemicals mixed. The room filled with an eerie chemiluminescent greenish glow.

He held the light aloft and searched the desk, rummaging through the books and papers: there were diagrams for an artificial bird, notes on the history of bi- and tricycles, and unwieldy tomes on every subject imaginable, some written by Barrington himself.

What a gallimaufry! Fox-Torrington rolled his eyes. He dumped the pages back onto the desk. Did Batty Barrington ever concentrate on any one thing?

Fox-Torrington pulled a bundle of half-completed letters into the light. All were addressed either to The Royal Society For Improving Natural Knowledge, or the Crypto-zoological Society. He grinned.

Better. He dropped the letters back onto the desk and resumed his search; Barrington must have plans for this upcoming expedition somewhere. The torn edge of a scrap of a familiar newspaper protruded from the pages of a crisp-edged journal. It was the auction announcement. A much-thumbed Bradshaw's Guide lay nearby. Pages filled with Barrington's scrawled handwriting captured kelpie lore; a neater feminine hand had noted train times. Tickets and a letter from somewhere in Scotland were clipped to the pages.

Fox-Torrington stuffed them all into his satchel. He scowled. He'd found nothing resembling the Kelpie's Bridle itself.

A clock chimed downstairs. Fox-Torrington checked his pocket watch. He must go, or lose his alibi.

He was slower making his exit; he hauled himself up through the skylight, padded back along the roof, and down the drainpipe. Crossing to the coach house roof, he kept low, remaining unseen should anyone be about and look up. He checked up and down the narrow lane, and listened for any carriages returning early. Coast clear. He dropped into the Mews, retrieved his coat and hat, and shivered into them, even though the night was warm.

Back on the moonlit street, a quick glance showed the Copper had not yet returned along his beat. Fox-Torrington straightened his shoulders and strolled towards his waiting carriage.

He re-entered the ballroom with one waltz to spare before honouring his dance engagement with Hermia Barrington.

Hemmy stepped from her room and turned to go downstairs to breakfast.

"John!" called Eli, from the attic. Hemmy glanced up. Eli must be at work already. His worried tone sounded impatient, and not like himself at all. She turned and started upstairs.

Hurried footfalls echoed from the servant's staircase, from the floor above. The footman's voice drifted down the stairwell.

"Yes, sir?" John sounded breathless but calm.

"John, someone's moved my journals. I can't find them." Hemmy trotted attic-ward, her feet whispering on the carpet as she ran.

"Was anyone in this room last night, or early this morning?" Eli asked. A drawer scraped open. Something thudded to the floor. Eli muttered a curse.

"Not that I know of, sir. All the house servants but Miss Carlin retired early, I believe. Would you like me to enquire?"

"Yes, John. And ask Mrs. Barrington to step up here, when she has a moment."

"Very good, sir," said John. Hemmy stepped onto the landing just as he closed the laboratory door. He re-opened it and stepped back, allowing Hemmy to enter.

"I'm here, Eli," Hemmy replied, "Is something wrong?" She stepped into the room. A drawing fluttered to her feet. "What have you lost?" She picked up a bundle of discarded letters from the floor and placed them on his desk.

"I can't find my kelpie journals." Eli rifled through the contents of his desk. Letters and notes and drawings spilled onto the rugs. "You haven't tidied, have you?"

Hemmy turned up the gaslight for him.

"Certainly not – I never touch your desk." Hemmy shivered. "Oh, it's so cold in here! Have you left a window open?" She glanced at the closed windows and frowned, trying to determine from whence the draughts were coming. Elias shook his head.

"Perhaps you put the journals in the safe with the bridle?"

"I don't remember–"

As he moved away from his desk to look, something crunched under his feet; he seemed not to notice. Hemmy looked at the floor near him.

"Broken glass! From where?" They both scanned the room. Hemmy spotted it first and pointed upward. "The skylight!"

Hemmy peered into the thin morning sunlight; there was a piece of glass missing from near the catch and the skylight had been left ajar. She bent and picked up a shard from the floor.

"Cut, not broken," she announced, displaying the curved edge. "Someone came over the roofs, climbed in through there, and took your notes. Is anything else taken?" She examined the room again. "They knew what they were after. There's nothing else missing." She nodded towards his flying machine plans, discarded on the table.

Eli yanked the pull of the servant's bell. Footsteps pounded up the stairs. Hannah and John arrived at the laboratory door simultaneously.

"John, fetch a policeman. We have been burgled!" Eli said.

John bounded back down the steps. Hannah followed.

"I'm an idiot." Lines deepened in Eli's forehead. "I never thought of criminal interest in my work." He ruffled his fair hair, and stared at the skylight. "We'll need bars for the windows and a new skylight. I'll order them today." He turned to face Hemmy and clasped her hands.

"Hermia, love, have Carlin pack your bags. You're going to the country house until this is all resolved. You'll be safer there."

"I don't wish to go, Eli. I'm staying with you," she whispered back.

Eli swallowed. His face paled. "A wife should—"

Her stomach lurched. "A wife's place is by her husband's side, Eli." She would hear no husbandly lectures. Nor would she be left behind.

"Please, Hemmy?" He kissed her hands; she felt his lips tremble.

Her heart sank. She hadn't realised how worried he was. Perhaps the expedition was more dangerous than she knew? She turned her head, and blinked away her tears.

Then Hemmy nodded. She wouldn't fight him on this. Not this time.

"If you insist, I will call Carlin to pack."

His arms encircled her, he held her for long moments. Eli ushered her from the laboratory and locked the door behind them. His arm remained around her shoulders.

CHAPTER SEVEN

Hemmy laid the last brown paper package with the other boxes on the bed. She looked over her haul as she removed her outdoor gloves and nodded. It'd been a very successful shopping trip. One needed so many new things for a stay in the country.

Carlin emerged from her Mistress's dressing room and helped her out of her coat. Hemmy removed her hat pins and took off her hat, handing it to Carlin.

"I think the ribbon is loose. Please see to it, Carlin."

"Yes, madam." Miss Carlin withdrew to the dressing room again and Hemmy heard the squeak of a cupboard door as Carlin fetched her sewing basket.

Keeping her eye on the door, Hemmy retrieved several small packages from the pile on the bed and secreted them in a hidden pocket inside the folds of her backswept skirt. One needed new things for a Cryptozoological Expedition, also. She patted the pockets, and smiled. Eli would not bundle her off to the country. She was indispensable to him, and she would show him she could look after herself.

She untied strings, removed brown paper wrappings and opened boxes. She shook out a midnight blue, full, trouser-like garment and held it up against herself. The saleswoman had called them "bicycle bloomers". Yards of material had been gathered into the waistband and knee cuffs. She screwed up her mouth. Should she have bought these? She didn't even ride a bicycle. Was she really bold enough to wear them, these bloomers? She held her breath. Yes, she must. She was determined to accompany Eli. Someone needed to keep an eye on him. She held the bloomers against her waist and let her breath escape. And she couldn't traipse around in a full-length riding habit.

There was a knock on the bedroom door. Hemmy dropped the bloomers on the bed. Carlin re-entered the bedroom, opened the door, and exchanged a few hushed words with the maid in the hall.

"What is it, Carlin?" asked Hemmy.

"There's another delivery downstairs," replied Carlin, "from your dressmaker, madam."

"I don't remember ordering anything else," said Hemmy.

"It seems it's addressed to *Mister* Barrington, madam."

"It's sure to be some simple mistake."

Hemmy descended the stairs to the front hall. The footman, John, stood watch over three delivery boys. Each struggled with over-sized parcels, all of which were well wrapped against the dust of the streets.

One of the thick, flat parcels slipped in the arms of the smallest boy, just missed a Chinese vase on the hall table, and thudded against the dark wallpaper, leaving a scuff mark.

"Careful there, boy," grumbled John.

"Sir." He re-balanced his load, and shuffled away from the wall.

Hermia approached the eldest-looking youth. "Are you certain the delivery is for Mr Barrington?"

The eldest boy nodded. "I'm sure, missus. Mademoiselle said to deliver to the *gentleman*. He bought it all."

Footsteps bounded down the staircase behind Hemmy.

"Is that my silk arriving?" Eli hefted one of the parcels and hugged it to his chest. "Excellent!" He beamed. "John, have them take it all up to my workroom."

"Up the stairs, sir?"

Eli halted. "Oh." He shrugged and waved a dismissive hand. "Up you go, boys."

"Yes, sir." John ushered the boys across the hall towards the stairs.

Hemmy followed. Whatever could Eli want with all that silk?

Hemmy shut the laboratory door behind her. The wrapped bolts of silk were stacked in the laboratory, competing for floorspace with two large, cloth-draped wooden crates, which must have been delivered earlier in the day. Eli tore the wrapping off one of the packages, revealing the fabric, streakily dyed in the most horrendous shade of puce. Hemmy screwed up her nose. No woman of style would ever be seen in such a dull, unfashionable colour!

Eli tossed the brown paper wrapping aside and grunted in satisfaction.

"Is it all the same -" Hemmy rubbed her nose, "*remarkable* colour?"

"Of course not." Eli chuckled. "Some of it's worse."

"What *is* it for?"

Eli picked up one of his models from his workbench.

"The flying machine?" She joined him at the bench.

"It's for the wings," he said. "The colour's irrelevant; it's the lightness and strength that's needed." He turned the model, as if making it bank on imaginary wind currents.

Hemmy bit her lip. She picked up one of his other models and looked at it. If he started on another inventing frenzy, he'd forget about his kelpie expedition…

That might suit *her*, but how would *he* feel if he missed such an opportunity? She put the little flyer down, and picked up another one.

She sighed. "But what about your kelpie?" asked Hemmy, replacing the small machine where he had put it. They had social obligations, too. Had he forgotten? "*And* we're invited to shoot at Alford Hall, next week. You can't start on that flyer now."

"Yes, yes," Eli muttered. "There's plenty of time." Had he even heard her? He rummaged through the notes on his desk. "Have you seen my drawings?"

Hemmy picked them out from under a pile of notes and handed them to him and sighed. There, he was off again, head in the clouds. A smile hovered on her lips.

Perhaps she should try her idea to combat Elias's problems with punctuality when he was working, today? She'd have the Dressing and Dinner bells rung one quarter of an hour early, and then again, on time. Perhaps that way Eli would least at remember to eat…

He took the drawings from her, looked at them, and put them down again. Eli flung the cloth off one of the crates, picked up a crowbar and levered the top off the wooden box. He pulled out some lengths of shiny metal and examined them.

Hemmy peeked over his shoulder. "Something more for the flying machine?"

"That's right. Your father calls it 'Vernium'; it's light and strong. Perfect for flying machines. I hope."

Papa authorised a shipment of Vernium for Eli? Didn't one need a Royal warrant for that?

Eli reached back inside the crate, drew out two envelopes and looked at them. He handed to Hemmy the one without the Prince Consort's Coat of Arms printed on the top.

"This one's addressed to you," he said.

"Me?" She opened it. It was in her brother's handwriting and addressed to *Hemlock Soames*.

Hemmy smiled; Jamie still called her by the childhood nickname he had given her. At age eleven, inspired by Conan Doyle's *A Study in Scarlet* she had asked to study science. Jamie insisted that although *some* girls became scientists, they could *not* be investigators. In his teasing, her name, Hemmy Soames, had become entwined with 'Sherlock Holmes', and he'd called her 'Hemlock Soames' ever since.

She unfolded the letter.

> *Dear Hemlock,*
> *I expect Elias has told you that Father suggests the flying machine be tested here at Inver Nevis when it is ready. Our Royal patron is anxious to hear of its progress.*
> *Why don't we all meet here, instead of at home? Write and tell us when. Make it after the shooting season, though, or Father will be livid. And he is desperate to show Eli the new manufactory.*
> *I know Mother would be delighted if you came for a visit.*
> *Your affectionate brother,*
> *James Soames.*

Hemmy handed the letter to Eli. He skimmed the page and grinned.

"Perfect!" Eli clapped his hands. "We'll test the flyer at Inver Nevis. Then I'll go on to Inverness, talk to McGregor, and search for the kelpie while you visit your mother."

Hemmy wrinkled her eyebrows. "That's not what I had–"

"Do we want to travel to Scotland by air or rail?" He turned back to face his workbench and examined the diagrams of his flying machine.

Hemmy huffed. Provoking man. The perfect solution, was it? Hemmy took a deep breath. Well, perhaps she could find some good in this plan. She'd wanted to see the new Highlands train. She let out a slow breath. Yes, in the meantime, she'd travel in style.

"Airship would be faster," mumbled Eli.

By air meant either by airship or slow passenger hot air balloon. The first was ultra-luxurious, and more expensive, so would not be as crowded. Airships were also safer since the use of the newly discovered and non-flammable helium had been regulated. And the train left more time for thinking, and for 'discussing' things.

"May we go by train this time, Eli?" she finally replied. "They've finished the new viaduct, and *The Albert Royale* is said to be a magnificent train." She wrapped her arms around his waist and rested her chin on his shoulder. "We can go by airship to Lord Alford's."

"The train it is, then," he said, not taking his attention from the Vernium rods in his hand "The train's partially constructed from this new metal. I'd be interested to see how it performs." His shoulders dropped. "But *must* we attend that dashed grouse shooting party at the Alford's?" he sighed.

CHAPTER EIGHT

White clouds drifted past the thick-glassed window of the airship cabin. The floor of the *salon* vibrated under Hemmy's feet. She tilted her head to listen for the engines. A soft chug was barely audible; the airship's engines were so expertly muffled for the travellers' auditory comfort. Nothing that could make travel more agreeable had been omitted by the designers.

Hemmy sipped the freshly brewed Assam tea, breathed in its relaxing vapour and leaned back into the soft upholstered velvet chair. The heady aroma of the fresh roses arranged on the table cocooned her. She ran her fingers through the thick, red silk velvet. She could imagine Her Majesty and Albert the Prince Consort travelling in such style.

"I wonder if the Queen travels by airship?" she said to Eli.

"Hmmm?" Eli's eyes were closed. He sipped his champagne, opened his eyes and smiled. "Every chance She gets, I would think." He stretched luxuriously.

Hemmy smiled. "You're going to purr in a minute."

"Me?" He lounged back in in the comfortable seat and raised his glass. "You're the one eating all the cream."

Hemmy shrugged, smiled, and popped the last morsel of scone into her mouth. Eli leaned forward and swapped his glass for a plate, and helped himself to scones and jam, too.

"I could get used to this," he said. "We should travel by airship more often." Eli took a bite and smiled. Hemmy nodded, poured a second cup of tea, and helped herself to another scone, which she slathered, with unladylike generosity, with thick Devonshire cream. She licked her lips. She would enjoy herself as well.

Eli chuckled and lifted his foot toward the table. Hemmy gasped. Oh, he *wouldn't*.

The cabin doors swooshed apart. An over-dressed couple stepped into the cabin.

Eli sat bolt upright. His foot thudded onto the plush carpet.

Hemmy hid her smile behind her napkin as she dabbed her lips. She took another bite of her scone; the cream was contrastingly cool and smooth on the still-warm patisserie. She relaxed into her seat as the airship chugged southward.

Lord William Alford's carriage was waiting at the Aeroport for them. Thunder rumbled in the distance. Lord Alford's footman glanced up at the darkening sky as he squirrelled their hand luggage aboard and bundled Hemmy and Eli into the waiting carriage. He climbed up beside the coachman, who snapped the reins, and urged the horses into a trot.

Hoofbeats clattered on the cobblestones until they left the town behind. They covered the country miles briskly, the carriage moving with hardly a bump, despite the unpaved roads. Patchy, light rain spattered the carriage as rags of cloud scudded across the sky. Hooves thudded on the earth roads and fell into a soft rhythm. Hemmy closed her eyes. Her head nodded onto her chest.

The hoofbeats faltered. Hemmy sat up, blinking. She peered out of the window into dimness. Surely, it was too early for night to be falling.

How long had she slept? How long had they been travelling? The clouds had piled up; the sky was now overcast. Instead of fields or moorland, trees edged both sides of the road.

The rhythm of the horses' gait had altered; that had wakened her. Something was not right.

The carriage rattled and stopped. The coachman's boots scraped on the footplate near the driver's seat, thumped into the ground, then drew nearer to them. Eli pulled down the window.

"Is something amiss?" he asked.

The coachman touched his hat.

"Apologies for the delay, sir, ma'am. It's Duchess; she's lame." The coachman's gaze caught Eli's. "I'll tend her as quick as I can, sir."

Elias nodded, and snapped the coach window shut.

The horses fidgeted. Then Hemmy heard it: something yowling.

She shivered, pulled her light cape tight, and leaned towards the closed window. Peering through the fogged glass, she looked into the dark woods. Eyes shone in the blackness, green and very large. Hemmy swallowed. Perhaps it was a very small animal... with very large eyes?

The horses whinnied. The carriage jiggled.

"We need to get moving," she whispered to Eli.

He nodded.

"Good lad, Brownie." The coachman's voice sounded calm. "Good girl, Duchess. All better now." He climbed back onto the carriage. It seemed to shiver in sympathy with Hemmy, as it rolled forward a few inches and then took off again.

Hemmy took a deep breath. They were back on their way.

Something patted Hemmy's leg. She gasped and opened her eyes. The eyes that met hers were not slit-pupiled, huge and green. They were blue-grey and human. Eli. Thank goodness. She smiled.

"Wake up, sleepy head." Eli smiled back at her. "We're almost there, Hemmy."

Hemmy's shoulders relaxed. She peered through the rain-spattered glass of the coach window, seeking welcoming lights from Alford Hall. Trees lined the long drive on either side; only a short stretch of pale road was visible as it continued ahead. A strip of moon-streaked grey cloud mirrored it in the sky, overhead.

A bend in the road permitted a glimpse of Alford Hall. It was long and low, older than her North Country childhood home, Soames House. Originally an Elizabethan manor with elaborate brick chimneys, the late Lady Anne had added modern Gothic extensions less than a decade ago.

Muddy water splashed the window as the carriage drove through the puddles in the drive. Gravel crunched as the carriage drew up to the front door. Servants snapped open umbrellas, scurried to meet Hemmy and Eli, and ushered them into the entry porch. The coachman followed with their hand luggage.

They entered a narrow, wood-panelled entrance hall.

"To your right, please, sir, ma'am," directed a footman, and they were guided through a wooden screening wall into the Great Hall. A welcoming fire burned in the Elizabethan fireplace. Clusters of armchairs and sofas were grouped near its light or around small tables, turning the ancient hall into a comfortable, spacious sitting room.

A powerfully built middle-aged gentleman stood as they entered, beckoned the coachman, and asked him in a low voice, "Anything?"

The coachman nodded. "In the woods near the Hobbs Brook." He bowed and withdrew.

A tall, dark haired maid whisked away Hemmy's damp cape and hat. Carlin, presumably, was already upstairs unpacking, having come down with Matthews, earlier, by train, with the luggage.

"Welcome to you both." Lord Alford's voice boomed as he strode across the black and white marble-floored hall to greet them. "Elias, my boy, good to see you again." He shook Eli's hand. "How's that father of yours? Nose in a book, still, I suppose?"

"I expect so, sir. Although the fish are running well this week." Eli smiled. "He thought you'd like to know."

"Did he? Good lad. Thank him for me."

"I will."

Lord Alford turned to Hemmy. "And this is Mrs Barrington?"

"Yes, sir. Lord Alford, my wife, Hermia."

Lord Alford kissed Hemmy on the cheek. "How do you do, my dear. I'm sorry to have missed your wedding. Out of the country, you know."

Hemmy bobbed a curtsey: "That's quite all right, Lord Alford." She smiled. "How kind of you to invite us to Alford Hall."

"Glad to have you. But not so formal – William, please. And may I call you Hermia?"

"Of course, Lord William." She sighed, glad to be safe within a friend's walls.

Lord Alford led them across the candle-lit hall, towards the central doorway into the screened passage through which they had first entered.

Eli stiffened, his face pale and devoid of expression as he stared up at the wall. Hemmy tracked his horrified gaze. On either side of the doorway the wall boasted mounted antlers and animal heads; trophies accumulated by generations of Alfords. Nothing unexpected in most country houses.

"What's wrong, Eli?" she whispered.

Eli indicated above the Tudor-arched doorway. She followed his gaze upward. On each side was mounted the head of an animal: one a polar bear, the other with a flatter face than the bear's, and long, lank hair, patchy snow-white and reddish brown.

"Impressive beast, isn't it?" Lord Alford's hand fell onto Eli's shoulder.

Eli flinched.

Lord Alford beamed at the trophy on the right. "All the way from Nepal. The locals call it a *yeti*."

"The Himalayan Snowman?" Hemmy slipped her hand around Eli's arm and squeezed gently.

"That's right," replied Lord Alford.

A door into the passage opened in front of them. A lady a few years older than Hemmy joined them in the Great Hall. She wore a handsome shirtwaist and tailor-made skirts, in the newest American fashion.

"Ah, here you all are." She took Lord Alford's arm. "Excuse me." Her voice dropped to a murmur. "Will, honey, our guests are cold and wet."

"Yes." He blushed. He cleared his throat. "Sorry," he harrumphed, "Got carried away."

The lady offered her hand to Hemmy to shake.

"Welcome. You must be Hermia. I'm Ottilie, Lady Alford." She smiled and shook Eli's hand. "And you must be Elias. Will has told me so much about you."

Hemmy raised an eyebrow at such informality.

"Formal introductions later," continued Lady Alford. "We must get you dry, then you can join us for supper, as you missed dinner. The staff will show you to your rooms."

The Butler led them along the passageway and up a spiral staircase to their chambers.

A warm fire crackled in the bedroom hearth and candles had been lit. Carved wooden panelling covered both the ceiling and the walls. A sweet resin-y smell of wood smoke met Hemmy as she entered. She breathed it in; it was so much more pleasant than coal smoke. The canopied bed, a relic from the Tudor era, was made and ready for them. Hot water and warm, dry clothes had been provided in screened off dressing areas.

Hemmy drank in the warmth, as she sank onto the nearest chair. Carlin folded the last of Hemmy's garments into a drawer and helped her remove her soaked boots.

"Ah, Carlin. What would I do without you?"

Matthews stepped forward and took Eli's coat, hanging it before the fire to dry.

Eli flung his damp gloves towards the chair on the hearthrug.

"That will be all, Matthews," said Eli. "Thank you, Carlin."

Hemmy blinked. Eli was rarely short with the servants, especially Matthews who'd been with him since he was a boy.

He paced in front of the fire. She frowned. Her heart sank. She'd never seen him so vexed.

Matthews and Carlin bowed and vacated the room. Hemmy locked the door behind them.

"What is it, sweetheart?" She took his hand in hers. "What's wrong, Eli?"

"I don't understand …" He paused and faced her, squeezed her hand. "To hunt for furs or food in need, yes…" Deep furrows formed in his forehead. "But to hunt a beautiful and rare beast and call it sport? That I'll never understand."

"I agree." Hemmy kissed his hands. She blinked back tears. "I think it's horrible."

He looked into her eyes. "Do you?" His eyes widened. He sighed and the lines in his forehead smoothed.

"Eli, the world is changing," she murmured.

"I don't think Lord Alford would agree."

"*We* are changing it. Lord Alford holds to the old ways."

"Yes." Eli nodded. "I suppose he does." He sighed. "Do you suppose he'll ever change?"

"Perhaps. If…?" A wicked thought occurred to her; she smiled. "The new Lady Alford is closer to our age."

"True." Eli raised an eyebrow.

"Perhaps if we made her our ally, she could persuade him?"

"I like your thinking. You have a devious mind, my love." He grinned. "Though perhaps we should introduce ourselves properly before we attempt to woo her to our side?"

Hemmy laughed. "A quick wash and brush-up, then, before we–"

"Join her for one of the Alfords' famous suppers." Eli finished for her. "I'm famished."

Hemmy nodded. She'd meant "brave the trophies in the Hall". Trust Eli's stomach to save the day.

The delicious aromas of hot buttered toast, fresh coffee, grilled chops, mushrooms, eggs, and ham, wafted from the breakfast table. Sun streamed through the bay windows.

Hemmy and Eli joined Lady Alford at the sideboard, eager to see what delicacies were on offer.

The Dining room door swung open.

"Good morning." Lord Alford nodded to Hemmy and Eli as he bustled into the room and joined them. "Good morning, my dear." He kissed his wife on the cheek. "You're up early."

"Yes," Ottilie kissed him and smiled. "I think I'd like to give this shooting a try."

"Do you really think you'd enjoy it, dear?" He said as he helped himself to kedgeree and a cup of tea.

"I shall find out," she replied.

Lord Alford cleared his throat. His voice softened. "Anything for you, my love."

Hemmy bit her lip. She couldn't leave Eli to face the shoot alone. She seized the opportunity to join the party.

"May I keep you company, Lady Alford?" she asked.

"Oh, yes. Please do." Lady Alford patted her hand and smiled. "And please, call me Ottilie."

The shooting party stepped out across the fields after breakfast: Hemmy, Eli, Lord William and Lady Ottilie, with the gamekeeper and the dogs.

The dogs raced ahead across the fields, or along the hedges, flushing any grouse they could find. Hemmy remained close to Eli, for moral support, although this informal 'shooting for the pot' suited him better than a larger affair.

"Get it, girl." "Fetch it up, Rufus."

While the dogs were retrieving, Lady Ottilie paused and checked her shotgun.

"You seem to be enjoying yourself, Lady Ottilie?" asked Hemmy.

Lady Ottilie leaned close to her.

"It's not that I think I'll enjoy shooting things, Mrs Barrington," she said, "And I'm yet to discover what Lord William enjoys about traipsing across the muddy wilds." Lady Ottilie smiled and dusted off her skirts. "But one does so tire of being confined to conversation at these parties."

Hemmy nodded. She, too, was weary of being left to amuse herself in the house, while only the men went shooting.

"I knew I'd found a kindred spirit." Lady Ottilie snapped her shotgun shut. "Does your husband shoot much?"

"No. He misses most of them," Hemmy replied.

Lady Ottillie's eyes widened.

Hemmy bit her lip. Her cheeks warmed.

"Oh, I didn't mean–. That is…" She took a deep breath. "What I meant to say was: my husband is a very good shot, Lady Ottilie, but I suspect he prays very earnestly that 'God will be merciful to the birds'. He's not keen on shooting as a sport."

"I see." She smiled and placed her hand on Hemmy's shoulder. "I like that," she said, with a quiet chuckle, "Yes, I do."

The shooting party straggled back to the house as the sun set.

Eli tugged off his boots as the gamekeeper took charge of their spoils. Hemmy had bagged two brace. Lady Ottilie, under Hemmy's instruction, had shot her first grouse. Even he had conformed to expectations and shot several birds.

"Never mind, son," Lord Alford whispered to Eli. "When you've been shooting as long as I have, you'll do better. You're always welcome to practice here."

"Thank you, Lord Alford. Very kind," he replied, avoiding Hemmy's knowing gaze.

The rest of the guests for the three-day party arrived during the afternoon, bringing their number to twelve in all. After dinner, the ladies withdrew to the Drawing room, leaving the Dining room to the men. Lord Alford opened a bottle of aged port and handed out cigars. Eli accepted a glass, but raised his hand when offered a cigar.

"No, thank you, Lord William: I brought my own." He patted his pipe in his pocket.

Eli sat in an over-stuffed armchair, stared into the fireplace and swirled the port in his glass. There must be some way to avoid tomorrow's formal shoot. Was Lord William offering any alternative activities he could acceptably take part in? Or...

He cleared his throat experimentally. No, dash it all, not a hint of a 'frog'. *Bother* his strong constitution. And he was no actor, to convincingly feign a cold.

Lord Alford lit his cigar, flicked the ashes into the fireplace and returned to converse with the other gentlemen. A footman appeared at the door, caught Lord Alford's attention and whispered something in his ear. Lord Alford puffed on his cigar and smiled. Nodding dismissal to his footman, he turned, spoke to one of his guests and beckoned Eli to join them.

Eli rose and approached His Lordship and the other man.

"You know Walmsley? Good. Well, Barrington, my boy." Lord Alford leaned closer and lowered his voice. "I've just had some news that might interest both of you."

"My Lord?"

"I've just received a report the 'Monster of the Moors' has been spotted. I thought we might see if we can bag it, tomorrow night. Are you interested?"

"The 'Monster of the Moors', sir?" Eli gulped a mouthful of port.

"They say it's some kind of lion." He blew a ring of cigar smoke into the air. "Damn thing preys on our birds."

Eli's heart sank. He was averse to killing for sport; he'd like to see the beast, but not shoot it. Or let anyone else shoot it, either, if possible. Surely Alford could spare it a few birds?

He took another sip of his port to calm his nerves.

"I should very much like to see it, sir," he said.

"Right, then. I've only invited you two, and Evans. We'll keep mum, though. You mustn't tell anyone, not even your lovely wives. We'll meet at midnight, at the north stables."

Eli nodded and downed the rest of his port. Now he just had to come up with a plan. Shame sabotage was not his forte.

Lord Alford inhaled on his cigar. Smoke trickled from his lips as he turned to the rest of the gathering. "Gentleman, I think it's time we rejoined the ladies."

Hemmy had followed Lady Ottilie and the other ladies to the Drawing room in the new wing. Several gas sconces lit the floral wallpaper: pink flowers entwined in blue and golden foliage. Ottilie's taste was unfashionably uncluttered: she had arranged to best advantage a few fashionable objects d'art alongside a Tudor harpsichord and a cabinet of curiosities from her travels.

"It's a charming room." Hemmy approached the large glass fronted cabinet filled with books. "May I look, Lady Ottilie?"

"Certainly, Hermia."

China cups chinked as Ottilie set out six teacups for their party. While the tea brewed, Hemmy perused the books. She pounced on *The Practical Physiology of Plants*, by Francis Darwin. That looked interesting.

"Do you take sugar, Mrs. Barrington?" asked Ottilie.

"One, please." Hemmy joined the other ladies at the tea table.

Ottilie handed Hemmy a cup of tea.

"I do like reading," said Ottilie. "Do you have any recommendations?"

Hemmy smiled. She knew she'd like Ottilie. "Yes. Have you read much Conan Doyle?"

"I don't believe so," replied Ottilie.

"Sherlock Holmes?" Hemmy prompted.

"Oh, yes. An exceptionally clever man, isn't he? Wouldn't it be fun to be him?"

Hemmy stifled a laugh and tried not to choke on her tea. She definitely liked Ottilie.

"Have either of you read *Tom Sawyer, Detective*?" asked Mrs Evans as Ottilie poured her tea. She ladled sugar into her cup. "You might enjoy it."

"I think Will—" Ottilie cleared her throat. "Lord Alford bought me a copy. He gets me all sorts of books."

She found it and offered it to Hemmy. "Would you like to borrow it?"

"I would, thank you."

"I noticed the antique harpsichord in the corner, Lady Alford," remarked Mrs Walmsley. "Do you play?"

"The piano, yes, a little," replied Ottilie.

"May I play you something?" asked Mrs Walmsley.

"Please do," said Ottilie.

After the ladies had finished their tea, the gentlemen drifted in.

Hemmy gathered up her book hoard. "Good night, Ottilie."

"Good night, Hermia."

Hemmy took her leave and made her way upstairs to her room, where her nightgown and slippers were warming by the fire.

Carlin helped her undress and collected the discarded clothes.

Hemmy sat by the fire. A late-night cup of cocoa steamed in her hands.

"Goodnight, madam." Carlin paused on the threshold as she was leaving.

"Is there something else, Carlin?" asked Hemmy.

"Well, Miss, not that you heard this from me," replied Carlin, "but the word below stairs is that some of the gentlemen plan to hunt the 'monster' tomorrow night. Mr Barrington is included in the invitation. I thought you should know."

"Thank you, Carlin."

"Good night, madam." Carlin closed the door quietly behind her. Hemmy stared thoughtfully into the flames, until Eli came in.

CHAPTER NINE

The next night, half a dozen men had gathered in the stables as arranged. Elias looked around; he knew both Lord Alford, standing by his big black mount Jasper, and Walmsley, to whom he was talking. That must be Evans, consulting with his loader about the gun. He nodded to him in greeting.

Two Loaders checked the men's shotguns, and packed extra ammunition. Grooms readied the horses.

Eli breathed in the fresh night air. The scents of hay and oats, horses and leather filled his nostrils. A young groom introduced himself to Alford's favourite dog, Rufus. Rufus' tail knocked the boy's cap. The boy laughed, pulled his cap down low, and ruffled the setter behind the ears. The men mounted up.

Eli stepped towards his horse. It tossed its head. The youth patted Rufus a last time and moved to hold the horse's head steady.

"Thanks, lad," said Eli, "but I've no need–"

"*Eli.*" The whispered voice was familiar. Eli peered at the boy.

"Hemmy?" He kept his voice low. "What are you doing here?" He glanced over his shoulder at the rest of the party who were readying to leave. "Go back to the house before someone sees you."

Hemmy stroked the horse's muzzle.

"Certainly not."

He sighed and swung into the saddle.

Hemmy followed suit.

"I couldn't let you go on your own, Eli," she whispered.

"If you're going to be a stable hand, at least act the part," he whispered as he urged the horse forward.

Hemmy chuckled.

"Just keep out of sight, and we may make it through the night."

They followed the other riders, and their dogs, keeping well back and out of their sight.

The moon rose. The small hunting party dismounted, and clustered around Lord Alford. Hemmy slipped behind Eli and held her head down. Rufus galumphed up to Lord Alford, sat at his feet, and gazed up at his master.

"This is where the beast was last reported?" he asked Walmsley.

"Yes, south west of those woods," replied Walmsley.

Hemmy remembered the green glowing eyes they had seen on the night they arrived.

"Right, we'll try this way–" Lord Alford pointed into the woods.

"And I'll go that way." Eli handed his reins to Hemmy. *Back for you soon,* he mouthed, and she nodded. You'd better be; just *try* and keep me out of the action…

"You'll need this, Barrington," said Lord Alford.

Lord Alford's loader handed Eli a lantern. What a strange design, Hemmy had seen nothing like it before. There was no candle, no reservoir for oil, no chimney or shade. If anything, it resembled an encased stout hourglass, filled with fluids. He watched Alford activate his, and then did the same: inverting it and giving it a sharp shake. A wisp of light floated through the device, followed by more. Ruddy light spread out. The red glow surrounded them for several feet.

Hemmy blinked, surprised her eyes didn't need to adjust in the lighting. These lights could be useful for Eli's expedition to Scotland. How were they made? And were kelpies diurnal or nocturnal? She looked towards Eli; he was too close to Lord William. She scowled. She couldn't ask Eli anything or she'd be found out.

"Where did you get these, Lord Alford?" asked Eli. "And why red light?"

Hemmy smiled. She could always rely on Eli's scientific curiosity.

"I had them commissioned for my last trip to Africa," Lord Alford said. "Big cats don't see light as we do. I'm told they won't see the red light, and it won't disrupt *our* night vision. Worked a treat."

Walmsley checked his pocket watch. "Back here in an hour?"

Eli and Lord Alford nodded.

They split up, a loader followed Walmsley and Lord Alford. Rufus trotted off beside his master. Evans, with his Labrador, Rex, at heel, set off alone.

Eli turned to Hemmy and winked. He raised the lantern and set off, moving away from the others.

Hemmy grabbed the shotgun from Eli's saddle and strode toward the glowing red light of Eli's lantern. The fool had gone off hunting, without his weapon. She checked it was loaded and took off after him.

The moon was high in the night sky. Its light turned leaves and branches hard-edged and silvered the moor grasses.

Hemmy waded through the grass as she trod the uneven ground next to Eli. The lantern tinted the ground near their feet.

"Is it really a lion, do you suppose, Eli?" she asked.

Eli shook his head.

"Could it be the creature we saw on the way here?"

"Perhaps," Eli replied. "I suspect it's a Scottish Wildcat."

Hemmy frowned. *Felix silvestris*? It was a long way from home.

Eli halted, turned to her and smiled.

"I saw signs of some in Wales," he replied.

"Wales?"

Something crashed through the undergrowth, and parted rustling grasses as it sped towards them. Hemmy spun, held her breath, and raised the shotgun. Eli raised his lantern and placed his hand on her arm.

"It's Lord William's dog." His voice held relief. Hemmy let her breath out in a whoosh.

Rufus tore out of a copse of taller trees at the edge of the wood, barking excitedly. He halted to sniff about.

Distant voices floated from behind him. He ran back into the copse, and re-emerged from the trees. He barked and took off past Hemmy and Eli, disappearing amongst a clump of scrubby bramble bushes in front of them.

Hemmy and Eli followed. They emerged into a small clearing to find Rufus scrabbling at the base of a rocky crag, too steep for him to climb.

"The 'monster' must be up there," she whispered and clicked the shotgun ready.

"Come here, boy." Eli's voice was firm, but quiet. "Here, Rufus."

Rufus looked at him, then back up at the rocks. He continued to bark. He'd certainly found something. "Hush, Rufus!" whispered Hemmy.

Rufus whimpered and pawed the rocks.

Hemmy swallowed; could she hear a low-pitched hissing sound? Or was it just the grasses blowing? The breeze felt cold on her damp forehead.

Eli raised his lantern and peered at the crag. A dark, shaggy shape crouched, outlined against the brighter sky. Its eyes burned in the dark.

<Go. Away.> A whispering voice echoed in Eli's ears.

"Did you say something, Hemmy?" He whispered. If he sounded threatening, he might frighten it into pouncing.

"No, nothing." She matched her low volume to his.

Eli shook his head; had he really heard anything? Perhaps he was letting his imagination run away with him.

"Has Rufus found it, Eli?"

"I think so," he replied.

Hunger pangs gripped Eli's stomach. It rumbled. He clutched his torso, willing it to stay silent.

<Starving.> The voice hissed in his head.

Eli swallowed. He felt hungry, too. And irritable.

<Go, barking one.> The silhouetted creature peered past Eli, down at Rufus. *<My kill. Mine.>*

Elias's eyes widened; his heart pounded.

"It's a *Cat Sidhe*, Hemmy." He grinned. Not a Highland Wildcat, after all.

Hemmy didn't reply. He looked at her. She hadn't spotted it yet. He tried to hold the red lantern steady.

"There." He nodded in its direction.

Eli frowned. Could she hear it? Didn't she realise what this meant? The creature was sentient. He took a deep breath. "Lord, it *talks*," he whispered under his breath.

"What did you say?"

"It's—"

A whistle pierced the air. It would have drowned his reply, if he'd even had words to make one.

Lord Alford's voice boomed across the moor: "Here, Rufus. Come here, confounded dog!"

Rufus jerked his head towards the wood, wagged his tail and sprinted towards his master's voice. Eli kept his attention on the crag, and the *Cat Sidhe* above. The rocks shifted below it; pebbles rattled downward. The *Cat Sidhe* crept down towards the hollow. There was a flash of movement in the red-lit shadows. The *Cat Sidhe* snatched at it. With a flick of its head, the dead rabbit wiggled in its mouth. The feline turned and bolted back up the rocks and over the top of the crag.

Eli lowered his lantern.

It was gone. The grumble in Eli's belly subsided. His heart took longer to settle.

Hemmy turned her eyes to follow the excited hound. He had taken the quickest way to re-join his master – straight through the tangled bushes.

She peered under the branches where Rufus had disappeared. His barking had taken on a distressed tone. It turned to yapping.

"Rufus is in trouble!" She propped Eli's gun against a rock and ran towards the sounds, ignoring her footing. Her feet slipped on muddy leaves.

Rufus whined. She pushed her way through branches that scratched and impeded her. Where was he?

The ground squelched beneath her feet. She paused to disentangle herself from a gorse bush. There, a few yards away, Rufus struggled, mired to the belly.

She pressed her foot slowly into the mud. It was not too deep, for her. She kept going. Her feet sank deeper with each step.

Rufus whined, as he struggled to free himself.

"It's all right, Rufus." Hemmy spoke to him in a soothing tone. "Good boy."

She reached Rufus, grabbed him, and hauled him out of the mud; a pain twinged through her muscles. She clutched him to her chest and ducked her head away from the affectionate greeting of his tongue.

"Hemmy." Eli's voice came from behind her. "Stay as still as you can."

"What's wrong?"

"The *Cat Sidhe*, it's on the big branch above you."

Hemmy looked up, not moving her head. In the branches of a wind-twisted tree, close to her, crouched a black shape; a large, muscular feline. Its eyes reflected green in the moonlight. It was the biggest cat she had ever seen, even larger than the Big Cats at the London Zoo. It hissed at her as it crouched. The dry sound was almost as deep as a growl.

Its striped tail twitched.

Hemmy froze. She struggled to hold the dog wriggling in her arms. She clasped his muzzle with her hand.

Behind her she heard the click of Eli's shotgun closing.

Eli stared along his gun.

<Do not kill.> The *Cat Sidhe*'s purring voice filled Eli's mind.

"I don't want to kill you." Eli lowered his weapon and heard Hemmy gasp. He glanced beyond the scrub towards the wood. "But others are coming, and they want to kill you," Eli said.

"*Who* are you talking to?" Hemmy's voice shook.

<The female smells afraid.> The *Cat Sidhe*'s tail flicked against the branch.

"She is," replied Eli.

"Eli, what're you doing?" She edged back and tightened her grip on Rufus.

"Stand still, Hemmy."

The *Cat Sidhe* eyed Hemmy. *<I won't eat her. Too much shell inside.>* It licked its lips. *<The small one looks tasty.>*

Rufus struggled to get free. He pulled his muzzle from Hemmy's grip and yapped.

"I'd rather you didn't eat the dog." Eli stepped between the *Cat Sidhe* and Hemmy and tightened his grip on his shot gun.

"Quiet, Rufus." Hemmy hugged the dog to her. "Don't, Eli, it's not safe." Her voice wavered.

< *Still very hungry.*> The *Cat Sidhe* pawed at the branch.

"I'm sorry, but no," said Eli.

The *Cat Sidhe* stretched one cautious paw downward and eyed him.

A dog barked. Men's voices came closer and branches snapped. A whistle; Rufus wriggled in Hemmy's arms.

Eli winced. "You must go," he hissed. "Run. Before the hunting party arrives."

The *Cat Sidhe* raised its head and sniffed the air. Its tail twitched.

"Now!"

The *Cat Sidhe* yowled, jumped to the ground and bounded away.

"Eli?" Hemmy's voice shook. "What the devil is going on?"

Eli lowered the weapon and turned to face Hemmy. Her eyes were wide, her breathing too fast. She released Rufus, and took an unsteady step towards him. The dog ran to the tree and sniffed at it.

"It's all right, Hemmy." Eli wrapped his arms around her. She buried her head into his shoulder.

"What were you thinking, Eli?" She looked at him and thumped him on the shoulder. "You could've been killed," she whispered.

"Never." Eli held her close. "An intelligent creature can always be reasoned with."

"Intelligent? You couldn't have known!"

"Until I *heard* it."

"If you ever frighten me like that again–"

He hugged her as they trudged through the marsh to firmer ground, closer to the trees. Voices shouted from the other side of the copse. The hounds barked as they crashed through the undergrowth.

Eli peered in the direction the *Cat Sidhe* had escaped, hoping it could outrun the hounds. He raised his gun and shot into the air.

Hemmy flinched. "Do you think it's gone?"

"I hope so," he replied.

The hounds broke through the copse's undergrowth, dashed towards them and sniffed the ground near Eli's feet, barking excitedly. A minute later, the hunting party emerged from the trees.

"Is that you, Barrington?" Lord Alford jogged toward them, his gun dangling from one arm. "Have you got it?"

"No, sir," replied Eli. "I missed, I'm afraid."

Rufus barked, ran back to the hunting party and dodged between their legs.

"Which way did it go?" Walmsley asked, striding up from behind Alford.

Eli pointed. Walmsley set off.

"Here, Rex, good boy. Sit," said Evans.

"He seems to be interested in that tree, M'lord," said one of the loaders. "Near the boggy ground."

"Evans, you take Rex and see if he can sniff out the beast's tracks. Try that way. He seems keen on it."

Evans ushered the Labrador toward the tree and they began to search.

"Good dog, Rufus." Lord Alford sank his hand into Rufus' fur. Mud flicked up onto his sleeve. "By Golly, but you're up to the eyeballs in mud!" He snorted. "And so is the lad."

"What lad?" asked Eli, as Hemmy ducked behind him.

Lord Alford's raised his lantern; his eyes widened. "Mrs Barrington?" His voice boomed.

Rufus dropped to a crouch and whined. Walmsley turned and looked at Alford. The dispersing voices of men and dogs stopped. All eyes were on Hemmy.

Hemmy froze. She looked towards Eli, and then at Lord Alford. The men wandered back.

"Lord Alford, I can..." Eli started to speak up. He stopped. He had no idea what to say. There was his wife, dressed in boy's clothes, up to her knees in mud, scratched, and covered in pawprints and dog slobber. She'd lost her cap somewhere; most of her hair had come unpinned and tumbled onto her shoulders.

Her eyes darted in Eli's direction. She winked. She closed her eyes, reeled and her knees buckled.

Eli stifled his smile and rushed forward to steady her. *Easy, girl. Don't overdo it.*

The hunting party gasped and ran back to fuss over her; gentleman, all.

Eli scooped her up in his arms and whispered in her ear. "What *am* I going to do with you?"

CHAPTER TEN

The clock ticked on the Morning room mantelpiece. A quarter past ten. Hemmy sighed.

Well, the little adventure was over, now. Home, sweet home. A few days of routine should help her to recover her nerves. She opened her book and stared at the words. She'd read the same lines three times and still didn't know what they said. She tucked a bookmark into the page, slapped the book closed and checked the mantel clock. Again.

The clock ticked louder. She glared at it.

She opened her workbox and picked up her embroidery. She stabbed at the linen, pricked her finger, managed half a dozen stitches, and dropped it on her lap.

This behaviour would never do.

She looked at her pocket watch. Eli wouldn't be back from the Club for hours yet. Hemmy rose, opened the Morning room door and checked the hall. It was empty. She smiled and ran up the stairs.

Hemmy closed the laboratory door behind her. She took her satchel from the cupboard. Her sketchbook and pencils were already in it.

She added small stoppered vials and envelopes for specimens, and a notebook, then crept back down the stairs to her room.

There she fetched the miniscule camera Eli had bought her and slipped it into the satchel as well. The small tools she had had commissioned for the Scotland expedition were secreted in her dressing table drawer. She unwrapped them carefully: a magnifying lens, a tiny but effective terrestrial telescopic spyglass, and a compass. She attached them to her chatelaine, next to the usual scissors, needle case, smelling salts, and watch.

Now she was prepared for anything.

The carriage rolled up to the huge fluted columns in the front of Euston Railway Station at twenty minutes to the departure hour. Hemmy peered out of the window, watching the bustle. She sniffed the air. The familiar smells of coal and steam made her heart race. Today was no ordinary day. She'd travelled by train before, but not on *this* train.

Her heart jumped. Her mother was expecting her to stay while Eli travelled north to Scotland. How was she to explain to Mama that she planned to accompany him? And how would she wheedle that with Eli?

Eli helped her out of their carriage. Matthews and Carlin alighted from the second carriage and scurried to find porters to help with the luggage. Eli escorted Hemmy inside the station.

She gazed around the spacious Waiting Hall. Coffered ceilings soared above her, supported by Classical columns. Two curving staircases embraced the statue of Stephenson. Passengers milled near the ticket offices and porters bustled on and off the surrounding platforms.

Hemmy checked the clacking Departures Board.

"It leaves at nine," she told Eli.

He nodded. They wove their way through the throng, across the Waiting Hall, and through the arches to the platforms. As they sat on one of the benches Hemmy gazed along the platform. Their shiny, royal blue train awaited. Its smooth and graceful shape was like a huge serpent, nothing like the chunky engines she had travelled behind before.

Two men pushed a larger crate towards the luggage car. Hemmy gripped Eli's wrist and nodded in their direction.

"Look, Eli, your flying machine."

"Yes." A smile hovered on his lips. Together, they watched it being stowed safely.

The station clock whirred loudly and struck the three-quarter hour. A porter guided an over-loaded trolley with the fingertips of one hand; it rumbled and hissed past them on its way to the first-class luggage van.

Further along the platform a tall woman in full mourning fussed with her black lace mittens and veiled hat as she scolded a young red-headed porter.

"I shall inform your superior of your ineptitude." Her voice resonated across the platform.

Hemmy winced; she felt sorry for the young man.

The widow turned to her Companion and continued: "Ellen, you will carry my dressing case. I don't trust this young imp."

"Very good, Your Grace." The brunette woman nodded and took charge of the case.

Her Grace turned her attention to another, stouter man.

"Young man, be extremely careful with my portmanteau." She stared down at him. "It's very expensive."

"I'm the Station Master, madam." He straightened his shoulders. "But I will arrange something for you."

He beckoned the red-headed porter and caught the arm of another youth as he strode by. He pulled them both aside, in Hemmy's direction. "Butter up the old biddy," said the Station Master, "and get her off my platform, sharpish. There'll be a bonus in it for both of you."

The two porters scampered back to Her Grace.

"Excuse me, sir." Matthews approached Eli. "Your luggage is in your compartment."

"And the flying machine?" asked Eli.

"Safely stowed with the portmanteaus in the luggage carriage, sir."

"Excellent," said Eli. "You're both excused until lunch time."

Matthews bowed and ushered Carlin through the crowd in the direction of the Second-Class carriage.

The Station Master returned along the platform, checked his watch and blew his whistle.

"All aboard!" His whistle's shrill note pierced the air a second time.

Hemmy stepped up into the first-class Pullman carriage. Her feet sank into thick carpet. She looked around her and drew in her breath. The whole width of the compartment was arranged as a gentleman's sitting room. Dark upholstered armchairs scented the room with new leather. Matching fringed curtains graced the windows. She hadn't expected this.

She looked at Eli. He was presenting the conductor with their tickets. The conductor checked the tickets.

"This way, sir, madam." There was a hint of a Lowlands accent. He led them towards their private compartment.

The Sleeper Carriage boasted a corridor panelled in gleaming wood; its decorative brass-work shone as brightly as gold. Sunlight fell through windows on one side, numbered doors lined the other. Their attendant unlocked their door for them and hovered near at hand, as they entered.

"The viewing Lounge is further along, sir. You're both booked for the first luncheon sitting and second sitting for dinner, if that is acceptable, sir?"

"Quite acceptable, thank you," replied Eli.

"Should you require anything, sir, this button will summon Service."

He pointed out the button near the frame of the door and gave Eli the key. "My name is George."

"Thank you, George." Eli slipped a coin into George's hand.

"Thank you, sir." George turned to Hemmy and bowed, "Ma'am." He closed the door as he left.

"After you, Mrs Barrington," murmured Eli.

Hemmy turned to explore their compartment. The plush seats looked exceedingly comfortable. Hemmy sat. She bounced and smiled. Crisp white linen antimacassars protected the seats' green velvet backs. A large window closed out the smoke and smuts of the station. Green curtains framed it. Hemmy leaned over and opened the fringed blind.

Eli opened the narrow wardrobe and put his hat away. A looking glass hung above the compact cupboard beside it, turning it into a dressing table. Another concealed a small hand wash basin with hot and cold water supplied. Hemmy picked up the small cake of soap and sniffed its lavender scent.

The train shuddered. Hemmy rocked on her feet, and she sat down. So did Eli. They looked out of the window. The platform slipped backwards as the train pulled out of the station.

Once the train left the city, Hemmy and Eli moved to the Lounge car.

CHAPTER ELEVEN

Her Grace, 'widow' Fox-Torrington entered into the Dining car with her entourage of one. A waiter escorted them through the carriage, and paused at a table. Fox-Torrington shook his head: it was not satisfactory. He pointed at a table with a better view of the compartment.

"Her Grace wishes to sit there," said Ellen.

"Very good, Your Grace." The waiter seated them, presented the menus, then withdrew.

Fox-Torrington picked up a knife and examined his reflection in the polished blade. His eyes were concealed by the heavy, black widow's veil. He assessed his surroundings. A decorative screen hid him from the casual view of the other diners. If he inclined his body forward a little, he could see the door clearly. He should be able to observe the Barringtons' arrival, and see if they left before him. He smiled under his protective veil. Just as he had planned. He placed the knife back on the white tablecloth, and nodded. Everything was quite satisfactory.

Hemmy and Eli followed the waiter to their table. The opposite chairs were already occupied. A stout elderly man in clerical garb peered over the top of his spectacles. The small, plainly-dressed lady next to him smiled at them. He stood as the waiter seated Hemmy, then both men took their seats.

Eli reached his hand across the table. "Elias and Hermia Barrington, how do you do?"

"Reverend Adramelech Cannon, and this is my wife." He shook hands.

Mrs Cannon nodded, and ventured a small smile.

The waiter handed Hemmy the bill of fare. There were three courses offered: white soup, roast beef and potatoes, and Port wine trifle, with cheese and biscuits to finish. When the soup was served, the Reverend attacked his with gusto, and no little amount of noise. She sipped her soup politely and refrained from comment.

"This is delicious, don't you think, Mrs Cannon?" she asked.

Mrs Cannon smiled. Reverend Cannon eyed her, frowning.

"Are you travelling to Edinburgh?" he asked Eli.

"No, we're breaking our journey at Inver Nevis," replied Eli. "I have business, and Hermia is meeting family there."

The Reverend harrumphed and returned his attention to his soup. He intermittently interrogated Eli about what line of business he was in, as he scattered bread crumbs across the table cloth.

"I don't much care for White Soup…" Mrs Cannon leaned forward and whispered to Hemmy, under cover of the gentlemen's conversation.

"No?" Hermia smiled at her as they both sipped the soup of chicken, veal, and almonds, "Which is your favourite?"

Mrs Cannon tilted her head and gazed upward.

"Cauliflower and cheese," she said finally.

"That's tasty, too," Hermia replied.

"What's that you say?" asked the Reverend.

"Nothing, dear." Mrs Cannon swallowed her soup and spoke no

more.

Hemmy gazed out of the window. The train's shadow raced across the limestone countryside. The rumble of the wheels grew louder as the train entered a long railway cutting and its shadow flicked up close.

Hemmy leaned forward; her guide book said that particularly fine marine fossils had been found hereabouts. Could she see any? The carriage's shadow sped along the rock face. She frowned. They were moving too fast.

"Do you travel much, Mrs Barrington?" asked Mrs Cannon.

Hemmy returned her attention to her luncheon companions. The waiter placed her main course plate in front of her.

"Only for the Season, though I would love to see the fossils in Dorset."

"*Fossils!*" The Reverend harrumphed. "Evil-ution! A load of scientific nonsense." He waved a forkful of roast beef in her direction. "God made the world in seven days."

"Yes, Reverend," said Hemmy, "But what was the length of those days?"

The Reverend's eyes widened.

"Scientists have recently calculated our days to be twenty-three hours and fifty-six minutes," replied Eli, with a smile.

"True." Hemmy smiled back. "And yet, the further one travels toward the polar regions the longer the days become. In summer, a day can last six months."

"Mr Barrington has just said 'twenty-three hours, fifty-six minutes.'" The Reverend's eyebrows wrinkled as he glowered at her. "Do you presume to contradict your husband, madam?"

Contradict? What was he saying? She frowned. How could one have an intelligent discussion without opposing viewpoints?

"Well?"

Hemmy's eyebrows lifted. She drew herself up straight in her chair.

Was the Reverend always this rude?

"No, of course not. I…" She looked to Eli for support.

Eli said nothing. Colour crept into his face. Was it from embarrassment? Or anger? She couldn't tell. This silence was unlike him. Why was he upset?

Her heart sank.

"You dispute the Bible, then?" persisted the Reverend.

If only he would go away… She wanted to talk with Eli.

The Reverend stared at her. Hemmy's stomach dropped. She'd only meant to contribute to the conversation. Pins and needles crept into her hands.

Eli frowned; his lips thinned. He still said nothing. Why?

Something cold and leaden rested on her heart; she felt it like a physical pain. She swallowed everything she was about to say.

"No, Reverend," she replied quietly.

"Then, perhaps next time you will leave the conversation to your betters?" grumbled the Reverend.

"Hermia." Elias avoided her gaze. "Perhaps you would like to retire?"

Hemmy's eyes widened. Tears pricked them. Eli could not have hurt her more if had he struck her.

She stood, walked slowly to the door, closed it silently and made her way towards their compartment. Her heels thudded on the carpeted floor, quickening with each step.

There was someone loitering in the corridor ahead. It was the tall widow who had been so unpleasant at Euston Station. Hemmy hesitated. What did she want?

The old woman stood outside the door of *their* compartment, peering at the number above it through her thick, black veil.

Hemmy wiped away her tears, and took a deep breath.

"May I assist you with anything, your Grace?" she asked.

"How kind," replied the Duchess. "My eyes are not what they were; the numbers are so small! Is this number eight-and-twenty?"

"Two doors down, madam. This is twenty-six."

"Ah. Thank you, my dear." The Duchess shuffled along the corridor. "They should make the numbers bigger."

Hemmy curtsied to the retreating Duchess and entered the compartment. The door clicked shut behind her.

She stumbled forward, seized a cushion from the seat and hurled it across the room. It did nothing to make her feel better. She flung herself onto the seat, buried her face in the other cushion, and pounded it with her fist.

How dare he? She gritted her teeth and thumped the cushion again. How *dare* Elias dismiss her like a child?

Tears ran down her face and soaked the cushion. Her breath came in sobs. Why had he let her down? He had always valued her conversation, and respected - even sought - her opinions. Her lips tightened. At least, that is what he'd always told her. Footsteps thudded along the corridor.

Hemmy relaxed her fingers and rolled onto her back. She took slow, measured breaths. The anger drained away as her breathing slowed.

The footsteps passed the compartment door. She let out a long breath and sat up. Her head throbbed.

She pulled her handkerchief from her pocket. A folded letter fluttered out to the floor. There was no need to read it: she knew it by heart. She let it lie.

She rose and poured herself a glass of water. The simple familiar act of drinking it calmed her. Why had Elias acted so distant? She'd only said…

"Ah." She closed her eyes. The advice of several Governesses echoed through her mind: *Women and children should be seen and not heard. A lady never draws attention to herself in any way.*

And she had revealed herself to be better educated than their luncheon companion. Hemmy's shook her head. And, by implication, Elias?

She understood now. She had forgotten the advice, and the Reverend had objected. Perhaps he felt that she threatened his authority? Or Elias's? Was that it?

And had Eli taken his outburst as criticism of himself? He had lost face in front of a stranger, and his pride was bruised.

Hemmy blushed.

There was a knock on the compartment door. Hemmy jumped.

"It's Elias." The words were muffled. "May I come in?"

She wiped her face, rose and opened the door.

Elias entered, turned the small dressing-chair around to face her and sat down. He smelt of tobacco and peppermint.

He'd been smoking. He only did that when he was upset. She bit her lip and waited for him to speak first.

"Hermia..." He hesitated. "Hemmy, I hurt you. I'm sorry." He placed his hand on hers. "Will you forgive me?"

She nodded. "Will you forgive me?"

"You've done nothing wrong," he whispered, "but I treated you shamefully."

"I embarrassed you. I'm sorry."

"I know." He leaned forward and kissed her. "I was at fault. I..." He halted, started again, "Not many men are used to an intelligent woman asserting herself."

He ran his hand through his hair. "Can you imagine how hard it is for a man to have a wife cleverer than himself?"

Can you imagine the difficulty of being thought, and kept, a fool, just because you are a woman? Or kept silenced by men like Cannon? She shut her teeth, trapping the mental retort; this was not the time for it.

"No," she said slowly, to give herself time to think. She squeezed his hand in hers. "And neither can you." She ignored his raised eyebrow. "Elias, you know you are an intelligent man?"

He didn't reply.

She swallowed. Perhaps he did not?

"Eli, I'm not an inventor," she said. "I can see what *is*, and make connections. But I can't do what *you* do; I can't see the possibilities of what can be, as you can. You have creativity, originality. I've always admired that."

His eyes widened. "You admire me?" He blushed.

"Enormously." Hemmy laughed. "I could never love a fool." She leaned forward and kissed him passionately.

"You know, Hemmy..." he said, after a while. "It occurs to me..." Eli blinked; a smile flickered over his lips. "'With the Lord a day is like a thousand years, and a thousand years is like a day'. Second Peter. Chapter three. Verse eight."

Hemmy raised an eyebrow. "Exactly. You should tell the Reverend." She picked up the letter and slipped it into her pocket.

She laughed and flopped back into the deep velvet upholstery. "Oh, I'm dying for a cup of tea."

"I must commend Western Caledonian Railways on their choice of teas."

Hemmy laughed as Eli opened their compartment door. A fine scented mist billowed out and enveloped them both. Hemmy blinked and sneezed.

"What the–" Eli coughed.

She placed a restraining hand on his arm.

"It's my talcum powder," she whispered. "Someone's knocked it over."

"It must've been Carlin." Eli chuckled. "She's probably rushed off fetch a broom."

Hemmy examined the room as the powder settled to the floor. Drawers hung half open and the wardrobe door was ajar. Several garments dangled from their hangers with their pockets turned out.

"What a mess!"

Eli pressed the service button to summon the attendant.

Large footprints marred the powder.

"Look, there's footprints. It's a woman's boot... but they are exceedingly large for a woman."

He peered at the floor. "With a very long stride."

They looked at each other for a moment. Hemmy edged into the compartment, tiptoeing along the walls to preserve the footprints, and reached for her jewel case, "It's been searched," Hemmy said, "but nothing's missing." She sighed.

Eli searched for the box containing the kelpie's bridle.

"It's gone!"

"Oh, no," she wailed. Had their burglar followed them from London?

Brisk footsteps approached along the corridor.

"How may I assist you, Sir? Madam?" George's pleasant Scots accent was calming.

"You may contact the police," replied Eli. "There's been a theft."

"I'll fetch the Chief Guard at once, sir!" George nodded and ran back along the corridor towards the guard's carriage.

Hemmy sat down to wait for the Chief Guard.

"I'll fetch Matthews to clean up," said Eli.

"No, Eli." Hemmy clasped his hand. "Wait with me, please. They'll have to wait until they've taken our statements and investigated."

Eli sat beside her, his eyes red-rimmed. He rubbed his nose. His gaze lingered over the spot where he'd hidden the kelpie's bridle.

Hemmy squeezed his hand.

"Is there another way to control your kelpie when we find it?" she asked.

Eli turned to face her. "We?" he asked.

.

CHAPTER TWELVE

Hemmy and Eli had commandeered the most comfortable armchairs in the Lounge for themselves. She closed *Northanger Abbey*, with a satisfied sigh. Miss Austen's stories were such fun; she had such a wicked sense of humour.

Hemmy stretched, and stood up.

"I'm going to fetch another book," she said. "Do you need anything from our compartment?"

Eli put down his pencil, looked up from his letter, and smiled. "No, thank you, Sweetheart. Unless you want another game of cards?"

"Or *you* want a game of chess?" She smirked.

He raised both hands, and grimaced. "I concede in advance." He shook his head. "I surrender."

His chuckle followed her from the compartment.

As Hemmy pulled her book from a drawer, the train slowed and halted.

Where were they?

She looked out the window. Only the first three letters of the station sign were visible.

She pulled open the window by its leather strap, leaned forward, and she peered out. Now she could read the sign: *Carlisle*. Not long and they would be in Scotland!

The platform buzzed with activity. Weary looking staff disembarked, and others in fresh-pressed uniforms with shiny buttons replaced them. Several passengers departed the platform in their horse-carriages, and a couple of new travellers joined the train.

A man, with spectacular moustache, and wearing a spotless white smock pushed an enclosed trolley towards the Dining car. A similarly-clad youth carrying an enormous basket of fresh vegetables followed him. The kitchens of the Dining car must be being restocked. Delicious smells drifted in in Hemmy's direction. Freshly baked bread... her mouth watered.

The rattle of the trolley stopped. The moustached man was talking to the widow. Or, more likely, *she* was talking to *him*. What could she have to complain about in the food or the service? Both had been impeccable. Hemmy sighed. Not her concern.

She made her way back to Eli.

The train whistled and chugged off.

When their train pulled into Carstairs, over the Border, Hemmy watched through the observation window as railway men uncoupled the hindmost carriages, and another locomotive was shunted into place. Her half of the train would continue North shortly; the other half would divert to Edinburgh ten minutes after that. Hemmy smiled; no more Reverend Cannon.

Eli was engrossed in the latest newspaper headlines. Hemmy's novel lay face down on her lap. Bustling, smoky Glasgow and the river Clyde were far behind them. Now the landscape racing past was wild and empty. Not a village, not even a hamlet. A stag lifted his head, gave alarm, and he and his harem of does fled from the train. Trees struggled up steep slopes. The train climbed.

Her eyelids grew heavy. She closed them and listened to the sound of the train's wheels. 'As-quick-as-you-can, as-quick-as-you-can,' said the wheels, as they dashed over the tracks.

"Excuse me: Mr. Barrington?"

Hemmy's eyes snapped open.

"Yes, I'm Barrington," Eli confirmed, "What's the problem?"

"If you wouldn't mind coming with me, please?" A serious-looking, moustached porter indicated the rear door of the carriage. "There's been a disturbance in the luggage carriage, sir. Some trunks appear to have been meddled with. Thefts have been reported. If you could check your locks and let us know if anything's missing?"

"Certainly," Eli pulled the trunk keys from his pocket and turned to Hemmy. "Excuse me, Sweet, I won't be long." He followed the porter towards the back of the train.

Hemmy picked up her book and read to the end of the chapter. She smiled. *The Sign of Four,* the newest Sherlock Holmes book, was just as exciting even on a third reading. She looked out of the window. Steep hills lapped against the mountains that crowded in around them. They would reach the new viaduct soon. Eli would be disappointed if he missed it. She checked her pocket watch. He had been gone a long time; he should've returned by now. The hirsute porter returned through the rear Lounge compartment door and cleared his throat.

"Excuse me, ladies and gentlemen. If I might have your attention for a moment, please?"

All heads turned.

"If there is a doctor in the compartment, would you please report to the Senior Conductor in the Guards' room." He scanned the length of the carriage.

No-one stood. No hand was raised. The porter's face fell. "Thank you for your attention." He made his way forward through the Lounge car.

Hemmy picked up her book again. Eager to re-join Holmes in his adventure, she turned the page. She hesitated. Shouldn't Eli have returned by now? A shadow fell over her book.

"I'm sorry, madam..." the porter began.

Hemmy's stomach churned. Eli? She placed her book on the table and swallowed.

"What's happened to Elias?"

"You husband has suffered a slight mishap, ma'am. One of the trunks shifted. He's asking for you."

"Take me to him."

She followed the porter from the Lounge carriage, past the sleeping compartments, to the back of the train.

"After you, ma'am." The porter opened the door of the luggage carriage and stood aside.

Hemmy entered. Chill air enveloped her. She shivered. She scanned the area; the only light came from the glassed half-panel in the door. Trunks, boxes and crates filled the space. But there was no Eli.

"Elias?" She frowned. "Where is...?"

The door behind her slammed shut.

Hemmy spun on her heel to face the door. The porter was gone. She rattled the handle. Locked. She pounded on it.

"What is going on?" she yelled. "Where's my husband!"

She turned and peered into the unlit carriage. A row of small clerestory windows ran the length of the ceiling; begrimed by soot and smoke they only added to the shadows.

"Eli?" She stepped forward. "Are you here?"

There was no reply.

Hemmy searched behind the nearest crate; the toe of a familiar boot protruded from the shadows.

"Eli?"

The boot wriggled.

Hemmy squeezed behind the crate.

Eli sat up slowly, cradled his head in his hands and moaned.

Hemmy dropped to her knees beside him. She held her breath and examined his head. There was no wound. She let out a slow breath. Her fingers searched his body for other injuries. There was something; a dart imbedded in his thigh: she removed it.

"Look." She displayed it to Eli. It was metallic, with a clump of red and yellow fibres at one end, and as long as her finger.

He nodded. "Help me up, Hemmy."

"Slowly," she whispered. She placed a hand behind his shoulder and eased him into a sitting position. "Who did this? Was it the porter?"

"I didn't–"

"The blighter has locked us in."

"But, why?" Eli mumbled and rubbed his forehead.

He hauled himself to his feet. He swayed with the motion of the train. He glanced at the closed door.

"Is the door locked?"

"Yes."

"What about the loading door? Or there must be a rear door?" Eli edged between the items of luggage and rattled the other door. "Locked." Elias said.

"Of course," replied Hemmy.

She wriggled past the crates, joined him and peered through the window. The track wound between steep, wooded hills. Even if they could break out, how far was it to the next station? And what might await them there?

The tiny hairs on her skin stood up.

The carriage shivered. The beat of the wheels on the tracks changed, its tone dropping.

Hemmy and Eli glanced at each other.

"No!" She peered out the rear door window.

The ground under the sleepers and tracks dropped away into a steep-sided glen. Water tumbled below them. Lines of shadow flicked overhead. She craned her neck; vaulted silvery struts arched overhead.

"We're on the Prince Albert Viaduct." Hemmy turned to Eli. "It's a hundred-and seventy-foot-drop to the valley below."

Eli didn't reply. He'd abandoned the window, and was examining the wall of the carriage.

She joined him. The wall was bare; purely utilitarian. There were no lamps, no decoration, but there was a lever. Hemmy tugged at it; it didn't budge.

"Let me," said Eli.

She stepped aside. Eli yanked the lever. It shifted slightly. Something thunked inside the wall. With a scrape, the wall slid several inches to the right.

Icy wind buffeted Hemmy and clawed at her hair. She jumped away from the vertiginous drop and pulled her jacket tight around her neck.

Eli slammed the sliding cargo door shut again.

"Our way out, I think." He turned to her and smiled.

Her eyes widened. "What do you mean, 'our way out'" Was he proposing they jump off the bridge? Perhaps the dart had muddled his brain? "You're not serious?"

She could barely hear the noise of the wheels on the track now.

"Eli," she whispered, "the train's slowing."

They pressed their noses against the rear window glass. The track was receding more slowly.

"The train's stopping," said Eli.

"On the viaduct?" hissed Hemmy. "Is the driver mad?

"Perhaps he's been taken ill?" Eli shrugged.

Hemmy raised an eyebrow. "Help me find something heavy; we need to get out of here." She rummaged in the boxes stacked against the wall. "Now!"

She found a small, solid marble statue. Eli brandished a sledgehammer. They advanced towards the forward door, separating them from the train. The train squeaked to a complete halt.

She struggled to keep her balance. Eli halted ahead of her and dropped the sledgehammer to his side. He turned towards her. His face was pale.

She stepped forward and looked through the window. Her heart froze. There was no need to break through the door. There was nothing on the other side. There was no train.

CHAPTER
THIRTEEN

The track was empty.

Hemmy stared out along the track where the rest of the train should have been. No doubt it was now speeding off northwards through Scotland without them.

She glanced up at the new metal girders, and stared down through the tracks. It was a very long drop into rough forest and brambles. Water cascaded over rocks as a burn tumbled along the glen.

Behind her wood thudded and scraped. She shuddered and turned to face Eli.

A pile of boxes and trunks been shoved to one side. Eli pulled a portmanteau from one of the stacks.

"What are you looking for?" asked Hemmy.

"*Our* luggage," came his muffled reply. He poked out his head from behind a stack and pointed on the other side of the carriage. "You try over there."

"What's the hurry, Eli?" she asked. "They'll come back for us eventually. The porter can find our luggage then."

He nudged another box and shook his head.

"Our train was an extra service. The morning train left hours ago. Our train won't arrive in Inver Nevis in time to warn them we are stranded on the track." He paused as if to let the information sink in.

Her heart pounded and her stomach knotted. She pushed aside a box of tools and searched the luggage on the other side until she found one of their valises, then their portmanteau.

Eli reopened the sliding door. Cold air rushed into the carriage, bringing with it the smell of coming rain. He pushed the discarded luggage out. Crates, trunks and packages tumbled out onto the tracks, or fell through the parapet. A smaller valise slipped through the gaps in the gleaming silver struts, and plummeted to the floor of the glen. A sizable area had now been cleared on the floor.

Eli slammed the door shut again and dragged a long rectangular crate into the cleared space. He snatched up the sledgehammer and slammed the corner of the crate. The wood splintered.

Hemmy flinched. "Eli!" She fetched a crowbar from the tool box and handed it to him. "Try this."

Eli levered it open. Inside were metal rods and wires. The patchwork silk filled the base of the box.

"It's your flying machine," she gasped. "My love, you're brilliant."

Eli nodded. "I've named her the *Kestrel*."

Hemmy picked up two rods and examined them.

"You'll need this." Eli handed her a cylindrical tube.

She slipped the ends of the rods into the connector.

Under Eli's direction, the framework of the Wing started to take shape. Yards of multi-coloured silk flowed over the floor. He slid the last pole into a channel along the edge of the silk and snapped it into place.

"Finished." He grinned.

Hemmy straightened up, smoothed the wrinkles out of her skirt and tucked a floating wisp of hair behind her ear. "What *does* one wear to fly in?" she muttered. No time to look for her practical bloomers.

112

"There's no time to worry about fashion," replied Eli.

"No," She slipped out of her overskirt, tucked up her underskirt, then pulled a shawl from their valise and tied it around her shoulders. Eli donned the warmer garments she handed him, then retrieved some goggles from the corner of the flying machine's crate. He helped Hemmy fasten them over her eyes, then fitted on his own.

Eli yanked open the side door.

She shivered. The chill wind caught at her underskirt.

Together they lifted the *Kestrel* towards the opening. The silk billowed and flapped.

Eli fastened broad leather belts around their waists, then clipped the harnesses to the flying machine. She lifted her feet into the foot rest.

"Ready?" he asked.

"Do I have a choice?" she replied.

He kissed her. "For luck," he whispered.

He lifted the front of the glider, ran towards the open door and threw the *Kestrel* from the train.

As the flyer plunged, so did Elias's stomach. He held his breath.

Dear God in heaven, please let this work!

He kicked a lever. The wings unfolded; their shadow spread over him. The glider caught a thermal, lifted and soared.

Eli scanned the hills and the horizon, searching for birds, for white cumulus clouds… any feature of the sky or landscape that would show him where the air was comparatively warmer. He needed another thermal draught to rise above the looming mountains.

A dark speck soared in front of him. A Golden Eagle.

Eli felt the port wing tilt upwards. An updraft. He smiled and shifted his weight, leaning into the thermal, banking to follow the eagle.

He let out his breath. His arm muscles relaxed.

Hemmy wriggled in her harness. He glanced at her and swallowed. She must be petrified! If he had been nervous about the *Kestrel*'s maiden flight, how must it have been for her? She had trusted him with her life.

"All well?"

She wouldn't hear him over the wind, but she might guess. She flashed a grin at him.

His heart pounded. Egad, she was magnificent! His throat tightened and his heart swelled with pride. He lost sight of his suddenly-blurred eagle guide as his eyes filled. Blinking, he returned Hemmy's smile.

He flicked his attention back to the eagle. It was there, just below them, and climbing. Beyond it, on the horizon, was a grey smudge. Was it rain clouds? Rain meant cold air. They must find a landing place. Soon.

He gazed over the vast landscape below and caught his breath. The river tumbled and frothed through the valley, occasionally flashing back rays of afternoon sun. Scots pines clothed the hills like dark fur, and the Ben loomed above them: ominous and majestic. White clouds scudded past the peaks, and the blue beyond looked endless.

Wresting his eyes from the scene, he searched the landscape below. A thread of smoke rose from between the trees. Hearth fire. There must be a farm down there.

A cluster of buildings sat amidst fields and rolling meadows. Scattered harvest workers moved back and forth, getting in the last of the hay.

Eli steered the *Kestrel* towards the closest meadow that looked flat enough to land in. The square of grass grew larger as they descended.

The workers lifted their heads and pointed at the flying machine.

The *Kestrel* dropped lower. Eli landed, still running. A jolt shuddered his ankles, but he kept going. He slowed the flying machine to a halt. The silk wings settled behind him.

Eli disengaged his harness and fumbled to release Hemmy. She breathed rapidly. Her face was flushed, her eyes wide and sparkling.

"You did it!" She grinned and planted a kiss on his lips. "Eli, we flew!"

Eli beamed. His flying machine had worked. They were alive.

He lifted Hemmy off her feet and waltzed through the grass. Hemmy laughed. He put her down and kissed her again.

Someone cleared their throat.

Eli and Hemmy turned to face the group of wide-eyed workers that surrounded them.

The grass tickled Hemmy's calves. Her cheeks burned. She stepped behind Eli and untucked her underskirt. The fabric settled around her ankles. She primped its folds until she felt more presentable.

"Good afternoon," said Eli. "Who's in charge here?"

"That would be me." A stocky, fair-haired man stepped forward. "Cameron's the name."

"Elias Barrington." Eli shook his hand. "How do you do? Mr. Cameron, we are in need your assistance. There's a train carriage stranded up on the viaduct. We must warn someone before there's a disaster. How far is the nearest telegraph?"

"There's a signal box near the village railway crossing."

"Can you get us there?" asked Eli.

"Aye. Y' can take the pony trap."

Mr Cameron nodded to a young farmhand. The lad ran off in the direction of the main buildings.

Thunder rumbled around the Ben. A chill wind gusted over the grass. Hemmy shivered.

"Come away in, lass." Mrs Cameron bustled Hemmy towards the stone farmhouse. Elias followed.

Hemmy savoured the delicious warmth of her tea as Mrs Cameron poured a cup for Eli. Heat crept out from her centre until her fingertips tingled.

Mrs Cameron put a stoneware plate before them on which lay two generous slabs of fruit cake.

"What were y' doin', flying around up there like birds?" she asked. "And the lassie with hardly a stitch to her back?"

Hemmy blushed. "We left the train unexpectedly," she replied.

"The line must be cleared," said Eli, "before the next train is due."

"Best be off, then," said Mr Cameron as he entered the kitchen.

"You'll be needing these, lassie." Mrs Cameron bundled Hemmy into her own hat and coat.

"Oh, thank you," she said. "I promise I'll return them as soon as I can."

They hurried out to the trap waiting outside. Eli lifted Hemmy up onto the bench seat beside the lad, and jumped up behind them both.

The trap rattled and bumped over the farm track. Hemmy clung tight as it swerved off the track onto a wider road and headed north.

Rain clouds piled up against the mountains. The wind gusted. Hemmy clung to the seat and clasped Mrs Cameron's hat with her free hand. She glanced up at the sky and hoped the rain would hold off until they reached the village crossing.

The village was little more than a cluster of houses and a sleepy coaching inn. Hemmy pulled Mrs Cameron's coat tight and readied herself to alight from the trap.

The lad drove the trap straight through the village and up the hill, towards the train track.

"There's the signal box." Eli pointed at small wooden building by the track crossing.

"Aye, sir."

Elias leapt down immediately the trap slowed, and sprinted up the wooden steps to the building's door.

The lad helped Hemmy down.

"Shall I wait, miss?" he asked.

Hemmy eyed the grumbling sky and shook her head. "It's not far to the Inn. We'll wait for a coach there. You best be home before the storm comes."

He tipped his cap and headed home.

Hemmy ran up to join Eli, in time to hear the signalman start tapping his message through the telegraph wires.

The signalman turned to face them both.

"All done, sir. All trains, up and down, are halted. They're sending an engine from Inver to retrieve the stranded carriage." He shook Elias's hand, and touched the brim of his cap to Hemmy. "You've saved some lives. Western Caledonian is grateful."

"You're welcome," said Eli. "I wonder if you would do us a small favour in return?"

"Name it, sir."

"We would like to let our family and servants know that we are unharmed. Will you send the telegrams?"

"Certainly," replied the signalman. "No trouble at all, sir."

"Excellent." He turned to Hemmy. "Hermia, I'll tell your father only that there was difficulty freighting the flyer, and that we plan to continue north. We can visit on our way back. How does that suit you?"

We? Hemmy smiled.

"Perfect," she replied.

The rain held off until they had walked to the village coaching inn.

Hemmy ducked under the oaken door lintel and followed Eli into the warmth. She sat at table opposite the fireplace, near the front window. Rain drizzled down the leaded window glass.

Eli chatted to the barkeeper and then joined her.

"The next coach goes to Bridgeburgh, but it won't arrive until well after supper," Eli placed two brimming ale tankards on the table. "How does venison pie sound?"

The fire crackled and danced. Hemmy nodded and closed her eyes.

The coach wheels clattered outside the window.

A rush of cool night air cleared her head as she and Eli left the inn. Brilliant stars glinted in the clear sky. Eli opened the coach door for her. The coach jiggled as he climbed in and sat down beside her.

He stretched out his legs; she mirrored his posture, and winked at him. "All ours, tonight?"

"As far as I know," he said. "Choose any seat you wish."

Hemmy chuckled. The coachman snapped the reins and the horses moved off.

"Outside, riding 'shotgun' for the coachman," she said.

"In case we meet a highwayman?"

"That's right. You'll be safe with me."

Oak and hazel trees swayed at the edges of the road. Shadows flickered over the coach. Perfect cover for a miscreant to lie in ambush. But suppose *she* were the highwayman?

Hemmy laid her head on Eli's shoulder and smiled. Now that would be exciting. She snuggled into Eli, closed her eyes and dreamt of the adventures of 'Flintlock' Soames, England's only highwaywoman, and her handsome masked companion…

Red tinged the night sky. It faded to brilliant gold. Ben Nevis and its fellow mountains loomed over them; the town of High Bridgeburgh slumbered by the waters of Loch Lochy.

Smoke trickled from house chimneys. Housemaids threw open window shutters.

The wheels of the coach rattled over paved streets.

Hemmy rested her hand on Eli's. He opened his eyes, sat up straight, and stretched.

"Good morning, Hemmy."

"Good morning." She smiled. "It looks like a lovely day."

The coach pulled up outside an inn. The driver jumped down, and opened the coach door for them.

"High Bridgeburgh," he said. "If you come in, I expect my Missus will find y' a cup o' tea."

"Thank you so much, Mr –." Hemmy glanced up at the inn sign. "Clarke."

Eli held the door open for her, and they approached the smiling Mrs Clarke, their hostess. He booked them a sitting room for the day; somewhere to rest while they waited for shops to open and made their new plans.

Hemmy ordered a full breakfast and pot of hot tea to be sent to them. They followed the maid upstairs.

She closed the door as the maid departed.

"What shall we do next, Eli?" Hemmy sat on a threadbare chair with intricately embroidered cushions. "Suppose we eat, tidy ourselves up." She brushed her crumpled skirt, "and find another way to get to Mr. MacGregor?"

"Good. Yes. Mrs Clarke says there's an Aeroport not far out of town. I'll see if I can book us places on an airship."

"And I'll inquire for a dressmaker," replied Hemmy. "There must be one nearby." If she was lucky the dressmaker would have something she could alter for her in a few hours.

She reached for her bag to check her purse: it would not be cheap.

A knock came on the door.

"Ah, there's breakfast." Eli rose and opened the door.

CHAPTER FOURTEEN

The Aeroport bustled: porters scurried back towards the Embarkation building with full luggage trolleys. Stevedores scrambled about. Across the landing field two massive hot air balloons slowly deflated. Teams of workers stood by to fold their envelopes.

Passengers crowded around the door waving their tickets at tight-smiled attendants, or scurried out of the rising wind, seeking shelter from the scatter of light rain.

Hemmy stared at the brassy sky.

The wind tugged at her skirts. She clasped her borrowed hat as she watched encoded signals flash from the turret to the stranded aero crafts and back, and waited for Eli.

He spoke with a sombre flight attendant. The gusting wind caught his words and tumbled them away before Hemmy could hear.

The attendant indicated the expanse of the swaying dirigible being secured by strong lines. It was clear nothing was flying today.

Eli re-joined her, wrapped his arm around her and guided her towards the Aeroport buildings. The doors closed behind them; within their shelter it was cool and quiet.

"All flights have been cancelled due to the weather," he frowned.

She sighed. There would be no making up for the time lost on the train, now.

"So how are we to get to Inverness?" she asked. "Is anything leaving town today?

He checked his pocket watch.

"The Loch Lochy paddle steamer hasn't left yet," he said.

Charles stepped under the shelter of the station roof and shook the large, warm raindrops from his hat.

The platform of Inver Nevis Railway Station was crowded. Charles glanced at the station clock. The London train should have arrived half an hour ago. He'd check for telegrams at the Stationmaster's office while he waited. Again. It was that, or buy another cup of tea; he already sloshed.

A shrill whistle announced the train's arrival before he'd reached the front of the queue. He stepped forward and claimed the telegram. Straightening the black band on his brown bowler, he tapped it back on his head, and strode from the office towards the platform.

Amongst the crowd, the Barrington's servants hurried off the second-class carriage and scanned the emerging first-class passengers. Charles scanned them too; but the man he sought was nowhere to be seen. There was no sign of the Barringtons, either.

Neither was the crowd thinning: only a few carriages or hackneys pulled away from the station. Guards rushed to the back of the train. Porters buzzed about with the organised confusion of an upset bees' nest. The Stationmaster addressed nearby jostling passengers.

"What does he mean, the luggage van is missing?" A woman in traditional mourning black and veil demanded of her maid.

"I'm sorry, Your Grace." The slender brunette shrugged her

shoulders. "That's all I know."

The widowed Duchess tut-tutted, and set off in pursuit of the Station master.

Charles read the third telegram and frowned. He crumpled it and stuffed it in his pocket with the others. They all said the same thing: Fox-Torrington had not disembarked from the train at Carlisle. The suspect did not leave this train at Edinburgh. Person of Interest not seen at Queen Street Glasgow Station.

He searched the crowd. Neither the Barringtons nor the man who called himself Lord Edward Fox-Torrington were anywhere to be seen. Not a sniff.

"Damnation," Charles mumbled under his breath. "Where in hell *is* he?"

A bicycle bell jangled nearby. The messenger got off his machine and pushed his way through the throng.

"Matthews? Telegram for Mister Matthews," he called.

"Over here, son."

Barrington's manservant. Surely Barrington would let his Man know what was going on? And wherever Barrington went, Fox-Torrington would go. Charles edged closer as Matthews read out the telegram to Miss Carlin.

Summer rain met them as they embarked at the pier on Loch Lochy. Drops pattered down, dimpling the water. Steep, forested hillsides cupped the lake.

Hemmy breathed in the sweet, resin-y, grassy scents of alder and Scots pine. The paddle steamer dawdled north-east up through the Caledonian Canal, and the lochs of the Great Glen. The worst of the weather held off until their vessel reached Loch Ness. Then it pelted.

She peered through the window shutters. Rain lashed the lake water making it difficult to distinguish spray from rain. Howling wind rattled the shutters, and rivalled the slapping of the steamer's paddle wheel.

"Eli, do you think we might see 'Nessie'?" she asked, using Eli's nickname for the creature allegedly inhabiting this lake.

"I don't think we could see her if she swam close enough to kiss us." Eli handed her the afternoon tea menu.

She sighed and relaxed back into her chair. She relished the luxury of breathing without having the air snatched from her lungs. Her hair was still damp from the downpour that had sent them scuttling into the salon.

Eli hailed a waiter and ordered a large pot of hot tea. And Dundee cake. Hemmy smiled.

Stuck below decks, Hemmy fretted. Every hour spent on the steamer was another their adversary had to search for, and find, Eli's kelpie.

She leaned out the window, stared at the still water and the shoreline creeping by, and snorted. She could swim the distance faster!

At least the rain had eased, for now. "Fancy a stroll around the deck, my love? Some fresh air?"

Eli shook his head, his hand pausing over the journal in which he was scribbling. "You go. I might join you later."

The rain cleared after two days. The sun gleamed off wet surfaces and sparkled off each raindrop until they were dried by its warmth. Warm breezes ruffled Hemmy's hair and stirred her new skirts. They spent most of their day above deck.

When they finally disembarked at Inverness, Eli hired a carriage to take them to their hotel.

A uniformed attendant opened their carriage door. Another loaded their meagre luggage onto a trolley and followed as it chugged towards the entrance.

Hemmy and Eli followed him toward the hotel doors, each one made of a complete sheet of glass, with brass filigree fixtures.

The doors swung open, seemingly of their own accord.

Eli escorted Hemmy inside. The doors softly hissed closed behind them.

She glanced back at the doors. Her eyes widened. There was no attendant.

Wisps of steam drifted down from the lintel towards the floor. She searched for a mechanism. Pots of semi- tropical flowering plants were arranged around the doorway so that, with each guest's arrival, the vapour from the unseen mechanism recreated the greenery's natural habitat. The effect was lush, exotic and cheerful.

"How clever," Hemmy whispered.

"The Scots always are inventive," Eli replied.

"Have our servants and luggage arrived yet?" Eli asked the Concierge, as he signed the registration book.

"Yes, sir," replied the Concierge. "Yesterday evening. Everything's ready for you, sir."

"Excellent. Thank you." Eli took their room key

It would be good to have her own familiar things to hand once more. And they could be civilised again. At least for tonight. Hemmy tried not to grin. What would Eli think of his wife wearing trousers? She slipped her arm around his. She'd find out tomorrow.

Puffs of white steam followed the luggage trolley as it chugged into the low-doored alcove by the desk. The porter loaded their bags into the alcove. It clicked and clunked. With a hiss of steam, their bundles whooshed upward.

Hemmy and Eli made their way upstairs.

Their suite was just as impressive as the hotel foyer. Hemmy washed in their private bathroom. She picked up a jar of bath salts from beside the bath, lifted its lid and inhaled. Roses. It matched the hand soap. Such luxury! She would definitely indulge in a bath this evening.

Carlin had unpacked and prepared her clothing for the next day: her powder blue day dress and smart, dark green linen walking dress, perfect for their visit tomorrow, and an outfit suitable for the evening meal. Matthews set out Eli's dinner suit while Eli washed.

Hemmy sat on the window seat and gazed out of the sitting room window towards the river Ness and the cathedral, then penned a short note to Mr McGregor confirming that they might call upon him the next day.

CHAPTER
FIFTEEN

M r McGregor lived on the outskirts of Inverness, in a gabled stone villa set back from the road and surrounded by landscaped gardens.

Hemmy and Eli walked up the path to the entrance. Eli lifted the gleaming brass doorknocker.

An elderly Scotsman in a kilt and faded jacket opened the door.

"Good morning," said Eli. "Mr and Mrs Barrington to see Mr. McGregor. We are expected."

"Barrington, you say?" The man's eyebrows crinkled.

"I sent a letter," replied Eli.

"Aye, there was a letter." The man's tone was a little odd. He rubbed his chin. "You'd best come in."

He opened the door wide and touched his cap to Hemmy as she stepped inside.

Eli removed his top hat. They both followed the old man across the hall towards an inner door.

Sunlight streamed through the windows into the Parlour. Firelight danced on the gleaming hearth tiles. Antlers and taxidermied animal heads hung on the walls.

Hemmy and Eli sat in the chairs opposite the small fire. The man then seated himself.

The portrait of a middle-aged man hung over the fireplace; an image similar to the man who now faced them. He wore a cravat and hat more fashionable during the reign of the late King William. On his lap he held the book he had presumably just been reading. The hand holding the book was missing a finger.

Hemmy eyed the old man sitting in front of them. All his fingers seemed to be intact.

"My father," McGregor whispered to her and winked.

"Please tell Mr. McGregor we have arrived," said Eli.

Hemmy raised an eyebrow.

"You can tell him yourself," replied the man with a smile. "I am McGregor." He removed his cap and bowed his head in Hemmy's direction. He shook Eli's hand.

"Now, what can I do for you?"

"Well, sir," replied Eli, "I wrote to you about an item that belonged to your late father, an item reputed to be the bit and bridle of a Waterhorse."

"The kelpie's bridle?" McGregor nodded.

"We were wondering if you could tell us about it?" Eli asked.

"Have you not spoken to your brother?" asked McGregor.

"My brother?" asked Eli. "He's in India, with the Army."

"Indeed?" McGregor frowned "But a lad calling himself Barrington came to me three days ago with the same request."

"But, Eli–" whispered Hemmy.

"He had the bridle with him," said McGregor.

"The burglar!" she gasped.

"What's all this, lass?" McGregor leaned closer.

"We were robbed on the train," she replied. "The thief took the bridle."

"And someone broke into our house and stole my research notes before that," Eli said.

She nodded.

Mr McGregor frowned. "You've not come to harm?"

"None at all, thank you, sir," replied Hemmy. "We were out at the times of both robberies."

"This false brother of yours is days ahead of you," said McGregor. "If you cannae catch up to him, he'll find the kelpie first."

Hemmy clenched her fist. She couldn't let Eli's work go to waste.

Eli's shoulders dropped.

"Is there anything you can do to help, Mr McGregor?" she asked.

McGregor glanced up at his father's portrait. "I can tell you the story my father told me."

He leaned back in his chair, thought for a moment, then began: "It was high summer. My Da was just a lad. He and his friends went swimming in the loch near the Stones. They had a grand time in the water. When it came time to go home, they hauled themselves out. There on the shore was a bonny horse. It was the most beautiful Da had ever seen. Its coat was as dark as the waters of the loch in winter, and it wore a silver bridle."

Hemmy nodded.

"The lads decided to borrow the horse and save themselves a hot walk home. My Da, being the smallest, was left till last. As soon as the older lads were astride, they were stuck fast to the beast. It dragged them into the loch, deeper and deeper. My Da rushed the beast, and his hand stuck, too. He couldnae free himself, nor his friends. So, he pulled out his knife and cut off his own finger. The bridle came away in his hands as the kelpie dived into the loch with a sound like thunder." McGregor leaned back into his chair. "The boys were never seen again."

"How terrible!" Hemmy's eyes widened.

"Aye, lass, it was terrible. But my father survived. And he kept that bridle till the day he died, always hoping to avenge his friends."

"And did he?" she asked.

"No." McGregor's gaze fell to the floor. "He did not. I searched the loch and couldnae find it. Perhaps it was the wrong loch. Perhaps the creature is dead by now."

McGregor stared silently into the fire. After a moment, he turned to Eli.

"Are you a God-fearing man?" he asked. "A man of faith?"

"I believe so, sir, yes."

"Then you should know that the beast belongs to the Devil himself. Do not touch his hide, nor let it touch you, for you will stick fast and you will never be free of him again. That monster will drag you into the dark waters, and devour you, all but your inwards parts."

Hemmy's heart plunged into her stomach. She pressed her fingers over her lips.

"My father was lucky he lost only a finger," whispered McGregor.

She glanced back at the portrait's missing finger.

"If the beastie catches you, nothing will save you but the Name of our Blessed Lord, Himself. It is a shame my father dinnae know that."

Hemmy reached out and squeezed the old man's hand; he patted hers reassuringly.

"It's an Ancient beast. You'd best use the language of the Old Religion."

"Celtic or Latin?" asked Hemmy.

Eli smiled.

"Latin, lass," replied McGregor. "St. Columba thwarted one of these creatures long before King Henry reformed the church. Though an Irishman, Columba preached in Latin."

Eli checked his pocket watch. "We'd better hurry if we are to catch our thief." He stood and shook McGregor's hand. "Mr. McGregor, you have been a great help. Thank you."

"Thank you." Hemmy offered him her hand, and rose to follow Eli.

"I wish you both God's speed," said McGregor as he walked them to the door.

Hemmy and Eli returned to the town centre, walking briskly, arm in arm. She relished the warm sunlight and cool breezes.

Eli approached the Concierge when they entered their hotel.

"We'll require some supplies for tomorrow morning, before eight." Eli scribbled a list and handed it to the man. "Have these ordered."

"Very good, sir." The Concierge rang the reception bell.

"And could you direct us to a reputable livery stable?" asked Eli.

The Concierge wrote down a name and handed it to Eli.

The next morning, Hemmy and Eli selected their mounts themselves, hiring two riding horses and a pack beast, then went in search of portable foodstuffs to add to what cook had sent with them for the expedition. They returned in time to change for dinner.

CHAPTER SIXTEEN

Hemmy assessed her reflection in the long mirror. The brown riding outfit trimmed with blue suited her warm colouring. She smiled and raised her long, full skirt to her knees to look at her matching bloomers hidden underneath.

"Shall I do your hair now, madam?"

"Yes, Carlin." The fabric settled around Hemmy's ankles again.

She sat and gazed out the window as Carlin pinned up her hair, then stood patiently as her skirts were arranged into flounces at the back.

Long shadows filled the streets as the morning sun peeped over the buildings and gleamed off of the river's surface.

The packs Carlin and Matthews had prepared last night leaned against the wall by the door. Hemmy checked her personal equipment while Eli dressed: drawing things, miniature camera, note book, and augmented chatelaine. All present.

After breakfast Hemmy and Eli made their way down the street to the stables.

Matthews was there before them. He fastened a saddlebag and slipped it over their packhorse. A stable hand checked that the packs were properly balanced.

Eli made a last-minute check of their food and tent. And the tea kettle.

"Did you pack the tea?" whispered Hemmy. She couldn't find the tea caddy.

"Yes;" Eli nodded as he inspected a box of bullets. Their silver shone in the morning light.

"What are those for?" she asked.

"Protection," he replied.

"Protection from what?"

Eli frowned. He managed a forced smile. "Just pray you don't need to find out."

Her heart jumped. She breathed slowly and deeply. He was just being over-cautious, wasn't he?

Eli dropped a few bullets in his pocket and packed the remainder with his pistol, then loaded his anaesthetic dart gun and placed it in a pack within easy reach.

The stable hand brought their horses out: a grey mare and a chestnut gelding.

Matthews held the mare's head as Hemmy stepped up onto the mounting block. Eli boosted her into the side-saddle and once she was settled, she arranged her skirts and positioned her foot in the slipper stirrup.

Eli took the packhorse's lead rope and mounted his own riding horse.

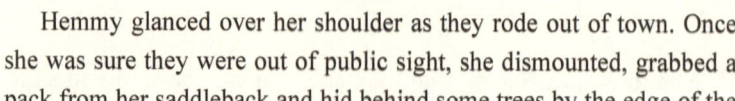

Hemmy glanced over her shoulder as they rode out of town. Once she was sure they were out of public sight, she dismounted, grabbed a pack from her saddleback and hid behind some trees by the edge of the road. She removed her riding skirt to reveal her new bicycle bloomers underneath, replaced her riding hat with a much more practical Tam O'Shanter and pulled on matching gloves. She bundled up her discarded clothes and returned to her horse.

Eli examined her new attire.

"What do you think?" she asked.

He smiled as he helped her remount her horse. He made no remark, but his eyes seemed to linger on her ankles.

Hemmy smiled back. She had her answer.

They rode along the lower ground nearest the river and the lakes. After a few hours, the land started to slope upward into moors. Then they headed south, as suggested by Mr McGregor.

Hemmy's stomach grumbled. She glanced up at the clear sky. The sun was just past its apex. Past luncheon. No wonder she was hungry.

She retrieved napkin-wrapped sandwiches from her saddlebag and drew her mount alongside Eli's. She handed him a roast beef sandwich with Worcestershire sauce, and chose salmon, cucumber and lemon juice for herself.

After they'd eaten, she retrieved their map and folded it down to a more convenient size to study.

"Where are we?" she asked.

Eli pointed on the map.

"There are half a dozen lakes to the south, and one to the south-east," he replied. McGregor hadn't been sure in which lake his father had encountered the Waterhorse, but Eli had been studying the creature for months. He'd have at least an educated guess.

"Which one do you think it might be?" she asked.

Eli put his finger on one of the Lochs.

"This one might be our best bet," he replied. "McGregor lived near there." He gazed over the landscape. "But it's furthest away."

Hemmy nodded. She studied the map and frowned. There was something… Something she'd forgotten.

She looked towards Culloden Moor to the east, and re-examined the map. There was a symbol near one of the smaller lochs. She closed her eyes. What was it?

"Stones!" There were prehistoric standing stones sprinkled across the moors. "Mr McGregor mentioned stones." She pressed the map into his hands and grinned.

He smiled back.

"Standing stones, do you think?" He peered at the map. "Or geology? The only set of stones marked in this area Clava Cairns." He handed her the map. "Druidic Temples. No lochs, but there's a river."

"Clava Cairns, it is then. We must start somewhere."

They bore east. The lightly-wooded land gradually sloped upwards. Wisps of white cloud drifted across the sky, looking like the tail of Hemmy's mare. Another wisp twisted like its blowing mane. The thud of her mount's hoofs on the earth could have been the thundering of turbulent white water.

"How long do you think it will take to find this Waterhorse once we're at the Cairns and the river?" she asked.

"Well, there are a few nearby lochs and waterways deep enough for it to live and hide in," he replied. "I suggest we build a camp this evening and explore outwards."

"Excellent idea." That's all they could do, since they didn't really know where to look.

"Race you to that clump of trees!" Hemmy threw a mischievous glance in his direction. She kicked her mount into a gallop before he even had time to agree.

"You trickster!" He laughed and pursued her.

They raced across the heather-purpled hills, side by side. Hemmy reached the trees before him. It was a clump of rowans. She rode under their shade and waited for him, listening to the bees as they hummed amongst the wild flowers.

The hoof beats of Eli's horse drew closer.

Hemmy leaned forward and broke a twig from the nearest tree.

Eli rode up alongside. She threw her arms around him before he could scold her for cheating, and kissed him, nearly unseating him. She pinned the sprig of bright red rowan berries to Eli's lapel.

"There! Now you're protected from all things Uncanny," she said.

"And what's going to protect me from you?"

They left Culloden behind them, walking their horses downhill into a leafy valley until the land flattened out as it approached the river. People had passed this way before them; a track, almost wide enough to be called a road, was worn through the grass. The Cairns nestled below, on the far side of the river. A narrow stone bridge spanned the water. They slowed their horses, and crossed single file.

Hemmy paused in the middle of the bridge, and looked up and down stream. Was any part of it deep enough to conceal a cryptic creature?

She urged her horse into a trot, to catch up with Eli. Here and there, solitary standing stones stuck up through the grass.

Surrounded by a copse of young beeches and oaks was the monument they sought: three hollow, round, stone structures, and several rings of Stones.

"Do you think they *were* temples?" she asked Eli.

"Temples, graves, houses? Who's to know? They meant something," he replied.

They rode past a man sitting on a nearby rock, a sketchbook on his knee. He glanced up and nodded a greeting as they rode by. A photographer stood by the farthest Cairn. His wife and child stood posed by the largest stone.

Hemmy's heart sank. This didn't bode well.

"No wild creature would stay in a place so frequented by humans." She murmured to Eli.

"I was thinking that, myself."

They stopped while she made a few sketches of the ancient monument - after all, one was supposed to be interested in such things - then they rode on, up out of the valley.

The moors steepened again as they rode closer to the hills. Water shimmered in the distance. A peak rose behind it.

"That lake is too far away from the cairns." Eli sounded disappointed.

Hemmy nodded. They turned their horse's head's and trudged back the way they had come.

They skirted the next loch. It was quiet, nothing but sounds of wind, water and wildlife were to be heard. She scanned the shoreline. There were no people anywhere. She eyed the water.

"How would we tell if there's one here?" she asked, as Eli helped her to dismount.

"See that water there." He pointed, his attention never leaving the water. "The turbulence?"

A stream fed the lake, tumbling over rocks in a small cascade. Hemmy nodded.

"Kelpies prefer turbulent water," he said. "And if you hear a thundery sound, it's the kelpie, submerging."

Hemmy listened for the thundery sound of the creature, but heard nothing but the splash of the occasional salmon, and the bubbling of the falling water. She sat down on the grass and waited.

The wisps of cloud thickened. The sun sank towards the horizon. Hemmy stood and dusted off her bloomers.

"It's getting late," she said. "Let's make camp."

Once they'd chosen a site, Hemmy picketed the horses, fed them some oats and returned to help Eli pitch their tent.

She breathed in the dusty smell of the sun warmed canvas, as she arranged a thick layer of heather under their blankets to make a mattress. The fresh sent of the heather flowers rose from the springy pallet.

A soft, rhythmic scraping came from outside: Eli was digging a firepit. Then, while he went in search of fuel wood, Hemmy drew a bucket of water from the lake.

By the time Eli had returned with another armful of firewood, the kettle had boiled for tea.

"Eli, where did you put the tea?"

Eli handed her a calico bag; it didn't feel like it held tea leaves. Hemmy opened it, and drew out several little muslin draw-stringed sacks. Whatever were these?

"It's my own invention. I call them tea reticules. Lighter to carry than the caddy."

"Sweetheart, I can't decide if these are quite ingenious, or just terribly funny."

"They're ingenious, thank you," he sniffed.

When Eli had shown her how to use them, there was enough hot water left over to made one of cook's cakes of 'portable soup' into a broth, which they ate with the last of their bread, and toasted cheese, for an early supper.

The crackle of the fire was comforting, as the stars brightened.

Behind them, the nearby horses munched quietly. Hemmy rested her head on Eli's shoulder, and looked at the stars. There was the familiar Orion. He no longer stood on his head as he did when Mama had introduced her to the night sky when she was a small child. She closed her eyes and remembered the crisp nights under southern hemisphere stars.

CHAPTER
SEVENTEEN

When Hemmy woke, the sun had risen. She sat up. Her hand brushed something on her pillow. She picked it up; a sprig of rare white heather, a powerful token for good luck. She smiled. How thoughtful of Eli.

The tent flaps stirred in the morning breeze. She peered out between them. Eli was already up, tending the horses.

She pulled on her boots and quickly dressed, laced up the tent and went to thank him for the flowers. They rode out again as soon as they had cleared up breakfast.

Their morning's search yielded no discoveries, so at midday they stopped for a cup of tea and lunch. Clumps of cloud shadows chased their airborne originals across the moorland. Grass and brush swayed and dipped in the breeze.

Eli stood to empty the cooled tea from the teapot. He was still for a moment, surveying the landscape. He inhaled. Hemmy, too, breathed in the refreshing scent of the heather, but detected no smell of water. The bracken at their feet rustled. Eli's gaze dropped to the ground. Hemmy spotted a flash of silvery tail disappearing in between the stems. A lizard.

He knelt and poked at a broken frond of heather. He didn't seem to have noticed the lizard.

"What are you doing, Eli?"

He raised his hand, and pointed at the ground in front of him. Pressed into the earth were three sets of paw prints: two small, one larger, with pads longer than any dog's. The larger prints showed traces of claw marks.

Eli crept forward, keeping low. Hemmy crawled behind him, until they crested a low bank.

"Look," he whispered.

Hemmy peered down into the hollow. Snuggled between the exposed roots of an old, twisted Scots pine was a den, lined with leaves from the surrounding trees.

In it were nestled two little creatures with the pointed ears and the muzzles of wolf cubs. Their pale grey fur, covering human-shaped bodies, was almost blond. Their hindquarters bore tails, but human-like thighs ended with long hind paws, and their front limbs ended in hands with claw-like nails.

"What are they?" Hemmy leaned closer. She remembered the silver bullets Eli had pocketed earlier, and hesitated.

"Not werewolves?" she asked.

"No," whispered Eli, "not werewolves. These are a much more amiable creature. They're called Wulvers." He raised an eyebrow. "I wonder how they got *here*?"

"Where should they be?"

"The Shetland Islands." He sniffed the air. "Smell that?"

There was a musky smell, mixed with something green, like wet dog, moss and leaves combined.

It grew stronger. A shadow moved on the crest of the hollow.

Eli looked up and scanned the horizon.

"There's the mother returning," he whispered. "I suggest we make a strategic retreat, and leave her in peace."

The next day they travelled further south and set up camp by a small, deep loch.

The light faded from the sky and the first stars came out. A fox barked once in the distance, and birds nestled into their trees.

Hemmy wiped dough remnants from her fingers. "It should be ready in about half an hour."

"Good, just in time for the stew."

They sat by the firepit, listening to the crackle of the fire and the hissing of the stew pan.

"One more day here, I think," said Eli. "If we haven't found any sign by then, we'd best keep moving on." Eli ladled stew onto two plates.

Hemmy nodded as she brushed the coals from around the iron pot with a green frond. She picked up a cloth and lifted the heavy lid off.

"Smells good." Eli licked his lips and held his plate ready.

Hemmy upended the pot onto another clean cloth and knocked on the base of the loaf. It sounded hollow. Perfect.

"How did you learn to do that?" he asked her.

"I learned a few useful things during my childhood, in the Colonies, too." She grinned.

After Eli secured their camp in the morning, they rode along the edge of a large lake.

Grass danced in the warm wind. A swarm of jewel-like creatures floated above a clump of flowering gorse by the shore.

"What are those?" Hemmy asked Eli.

He glanced in the direction she indicated. "Pseudo-Anisoptera," he replied.

She wrinkled her nose at him. "I knew that," she fibbed.

Eli chuckled. "Devil's Needles," he said.

"How pretty they are!" She smiled and edged her horse closer. "They look like dragon flies."

He tugged on her horse's reins.

"Appearances can be deceptive," he said. "They'll give you a nasty bite, given the chance."

"Oh, pooh." She huffed and continued forward.

Water splashed beside them. Eli scanned the loch, and lifted his field glasses to his eyes to look at two shapes moving in the water. Could they be kelpies? Perhaps a mother with a foal? Or just seals? It was hard to see. He refocused the lenses. Perhaps it was just floating driftwood.

He lowered his field glasses and turned back to Hemmy.

"It's noth–"

She was gone.

The glittering insects drifted upward in a cloud as Hemmy's horse neared the swarm.

"Too close, Hemmy!" he shouted.

"Ouch!" Hemmy slapped at her hand.

He winced. One must have bitten her. He rode forward.

Hemmy's horse danced and snorted. The insects hovered around them both. The mare flung up her head, protested and bolted along the shore.

"Hemmy!"

Startled grouse burst out of the old growth of heather, their wings whirring like machinery. The swimming creatures dived below the surface of the water.

Eli rode after her.

Wood cracked to his right. A man exploded out of the cover of the brush.

Eli's horse reared.

144

"You idiots!" growled the man. "You made me lose my shot!"

"Sorry." Eli turned his sidling horse to face the newcomer.

The birdwatcher's face was as red as his hair and his bristling eyebrows. He wore a tweed Norfolk jacket and brandished a long cylindrical box emitting wisps of steam from the disk-like structure at its front.

He stared past Eli, and peered westward across the loch.

Eli frowned. The birds had taken off northward. Why, then, was the birdwatcher's attention focused on the loch?

"Eli!" Hemmy's voice was faint in the distance.

There was no time to ponder the conundrum. Hemmy needed him. He released the packhorse, and spurred his horse after her, dashing in the direction of her voice.

CHAPTER EIGHTEEN

Hemmy kept her head and let her terrified mare run. She pressed her right calf against the saddle and her left thigh into its leaping pommel, securing her seat, just as she did when riding in the hunt.

Finally, the horse calmed and slowed to a canter, a trot, a walk. She reined the mare in. Hemmy shook. Her muscles ached. The horse twitched. She struggled to dismount unassisted, cursing the side-saddle.

She held the horse's bridle firmly as she stretched her legs, and murmured reassurances to the mare.

Sounds of splashing came from the waters of the loch. Hemmy tensed and searched the glittering surface. What was it? A large animal? A swimmer in distress?

Whatever it was, it was moving closer to land. It paused some yards from the shore.

It stood and waded towards her, the water becoming shallower as it neared.

A human figure.

Hemmy's heart fluttered.

A man.

Water weeds clung to his torso. Water drained from his mane of dark hair, his bare shoulders, his chest. He was broader in the shoulders than Eli, and just as well muscled. A silver chain about his neck shone in the sunlight. His large, dark grey eyes turned in her direction. Her heart raced. She'd read stories about people being enthralled by the gaze of magical creatures...

Hemmy shook her head: this was no magical creature. It was a man. She could keep a tight rein on herself. She was a grown wom –

She swallowed. That wasn't helping. Logic. That's what was needed. She took a deep breath. What is he doing here? If he had fallen from a boat he would be clothed. If out for a swim...

She cleared her throat. Certainly, bathing attire would have prevented this kind of delicate situation?

He paced through the peaty water towards the shore. The waterline encircled him and descended.

Hemmy's heart pounded. He might not be only *half* naked. Her cheeks burned. The heat crept down her neck and pulsed through her body. She slipped behind the mare, putting it between herself and the beautiful young man.

"Are you in need of assistance, sir?" Her voice croaked.

He reached out his hands towards her. The gesture seemed more an invitation, than plea for assistance. He stepped closer. He didn't appear injured. He was perfect.

Mist crept around her, enveloped her vision, invaded her thoughts. Her feet took a hesitant step forward, towards him. Without her permission.

She reached for his webbed hands.

Hoofbeats thundered along the track toward her.

Hemmy glanced over her shoulder. It was Eli. His horse danced as he leapt from the saddle, dart pistol in hand.

"Hemmy, keep away from that creature," he hissed. "Don't let it touch you!"

She hesitated. The sound of splashing water drew her attention back to the graceful creature.

Its perfectly-muscled arms reached out for her.

She smiled and closed her eyes.

"Hemmy!" Eli's voice was forceful, yet calm.

She shook her head, opened her eyes and backed away from it.

The creature bellowed in rage. It growled, the sound turning to a neigh of anger. It snarled at Eli. Its teeth were the sharp, pointed teeth of a carnivore.

She shuddered and backed away, toward Eli.

The creature's eyes were now black; he loomed above her. He raised his fists; they became the pawing, flailing hoofs of an enraged horse.

Eli lunged in front of Hemmy, pushed her away from the water, and raised his dart pistol.

Hiss...

The dart hit home with a sickening thunk. The creature screamed, then twisted and lashed out. Its hoof smashed into Eli's shoulder.

Eli staggered back.

The beast spun and plunged back to the water, and was gone.

"Eli!" Hemmy shook her head to clear the fog. "Are you all right?"

He stifled a groan and nodded.

She raced to his side.

"You're hurt." She struggled to catch her breath as she helped him towards his horse.

"Was that the–?" she whispered.

"Kelpie," he whispered. "Yes."

"But it looked so–"

"Human?" Eli nodded. "It's a shape shifter, remember?"

"Eli, I–" Hemmy bit her tongue. How much had he seen? She helped him into the saddle. "Let's get you back to camp. That shoulder needs attention."

The sun was low on the horizon by the time Hemmy and Eli returned to camp.

Hemmy sat Eli down on a log and retrieved the medicaments box out of her pack in the tent. "Let me see that shoulder."

She carefully removed Eli's jacket, slipped off his shirt and examined his shoulder. The skin was purpling with a large U-shaped bruise. She winced and applied Arnica salve and a bandage.

"Shall I get you the laudanum? I brought some."

"No need." Eli kissed her briefly. "Thank you."

His gaze ran over her forearms and neck. He took a bottle of calamine lotion from the box and applied the soothing pink liquid to Hemmy's Devil's Needle bites, then to his own. She dabbed the bites on his back that he couldn't reach.

"At least now we know the creature is real." She waited for a moment.

He didn't reply. She continued to dab the bite wounds.

"And we know where it lives." She paused. "It was a kelpie, wasn't it?"

Eli nodded slowly.

"Then we can go home. You can report to the Royal Society and everything will be back to normal."

"We don't have enough empirical evidence for a report to the Society," he whispered. "We'll have to try again." He swallowed. "We'll follow it around to the far side of the lake tomorrow."

"Are you sure?"

Nickering sounds came from the horses; the pack pony had re-joined them.

Eli yawned. "Let's tend the horses and then call it a night."

Hemmy nodded, and rose slowly. As she followed him past the

firepit, she noticed something draped over the log on the other side, something dark and wet and shiny. Her nose wrinkled.

Eli raised his hand to stop her.

"What is it?" she asked.

"I think it's a liver." He peered closer. "Deer, by the size of it."

"What's it doing here?"

Hemmy looked over his shoulder. There was still enough sun light for her to see paw prints around the cooking area. Wulver pawprints. And drag marks from the direction of the lake.

"Look," She pointed to one bloody pawprint on the log. It looked as though it had been made deliberately.

She clasped Eli's arm and scanned the horizon. A crouched figure watched them and raised a forelimb in greeting. Its eyes glinted light blue.

"There." Hemmy pointed to the Wulver.

"I wonder why she's left us this," murmured Eli. "A food offering? Perhaps to thank us for not disturbing her young?"

Hemmy eyed the Wulver. "But she needs it more, to feed her babies." She dropped her voice to a discrete whisper, "I hope she doesn't expect us to eat it."

"Perhaps with fried onions, tarragon and capers?" Eli smiled, "And tomatoes."

Hemmy raised an eyebrow and smiled. Her shoulders relaxed. Eli seemed more himself again. She indicated the drag marks.

"She dragged it up from the lake." Hemmy tensed. "I think it's a warning: The kelpie is nearby and is still hunting." She nodded in the Wulver's direction. "We understand. Thank you."

The Wulver inclined her head, turned, and disappeared into the cover of the trees.

Hemmy stared at the canvas ceiling of the tent. She turned over and pummelled her pillow. It made no difference.

"Hemmy?" Eli whispered in the dark. "Can't you sleep?"

"No." she said, "Can't you?"

He chuckled, rolled over to face her, and brushed her hair back from her temples. A tear slid down her face.

"Hemmy, darling, what is it?"

"That creature…" She drew a ragged breath. "Oh, Eli. If it had kicked you in the chest…" She sniffed. "A blow like that could have stopped your heart."

"Well, it didn't, thank God. It's only bruises, love. I'm all right."

"I love you," she whispered.

"I should hope so." He smiled.

"I don't know what I'd–" He placed his finger on her lips.

"And I love you, Hemmy." He kissed her on the forehead. "I am here, alive. It takes more than that to stop me."

She shook her head.

"No? Tell me," he said.

"I can't forget. I keep thinking about…" She avoided his gaze. "*Him*."

Hemmy's cheeks burned. She pressed her face into the pillow so he wouldn't see.

"You had no choice," he whispered. "If the kelpie had been a female, I would've fallen under its thrall, just as you did."

"But it wasn't."

"No." He stroked her hair. "The creature lures its prey like a carnivorous plant. It hunts by manipulating people's feelings."

Hemmy didn't reply. She laid her head on his chest, so he couldn't see her face. He kissed her hair.

"I trust you," he whispered.

She twined her fingers in his hair, and drew his face towards hers. "I'll never betray you."

A howl woke them. The horses stomped and whinnied. Hemmy sat up and grabbed her nightgown. Eli jumped up and pulled on his trousers.

Something moved outside. A shadow fell across their tent; the shape of a tall man, distorted by the curves of the canvass. Eli held his finger to his lips and reached for his pistol.

"My kelpie!" gasped Hemmy.

Eli winced.

He caught her by the arm as she rushed towards the exit of the tent.

"Wait for me," he said.

Hemmy halted and shook her head.

"What if it's our thief?" she hissed. "And he wants to get his hands on our kelpie?"

Eli frowned. "Stay here." He lifted the tent flap and slipped outside.

The shadow circled the tent in Eli's direction, something in its hands.

"Eli?" she whispered. She couldn't leave him alone. She scanned the tent for a weapon. She pulled a skirt on over her nightgown and followed him.

Eli lifted his pistol and examined the camp. The moon, waning, but bright, made the shadows confusing. He moved towards the lake quietly, listening for any sounds of movement. Whoever had been lurking was gone. Large boot prints dinted the mud of the lakeshore, leading towards the loch and away again. There were no hoofprints. He sighed with relief.

There was a splash.

He flicked his pistol in the direction of the loch. Something lay in the water, stirring in the waves. He edged closer. Dark shadows floated on the surface. The stench of offal wafted towards him. He screwed up his nose. It was the remains of the kelpie's last hunt. The creature had not come ashore to eat; it was still hiding somewhere in the depths.

Now their adversary knew this was the right lake in which to search.

Eli glanced back towards the camp.

"Damnation." He hurried back to their tent.

Hemmy stood by the fire place, an iron cooking pan gripped in one hand.

"Hemmy?" whispered Eli. "You should've stayed in the tent."

"I wasn't going to let you face the intruder alone," she replied.

"There's no one here, now." Eli wrapped his arm around her and escorted her back into the tent.

Eli found a sheltered clearing on a slope overlooking the loch, within easy walking of the western shore. Three standing stones rose from the grass: McGregor's memory was accurate. Eli set up camp, and collected wood for a fire. Hemmy unpacked the kelpie-catching gear.

They headed down towards the loch.

Eli scanned the area with his field glasses. Patchy clouds scudded over a cool blue sky. The loch was calm and empty. Hemmy joined him, unclipped a small telescope from her chatelaine and peered over the water.

"I'll search for footprints," said Eli. "You keep watch."

He wandered further along the shore and dropped to one knee in the mud. There were several inverted hoofprints. He smiled.

"Here," he called to Hemmy.

Hemmy withdrew her miniature camera from her pocket and took several pictures of the marks.

Water lapped the edge of the footprints, erasing them. "Botheration," whispered Eli.

"What's wrong?" asked Hemmy.

"We'll need to preserve these footprints as soon as possible," he replied.

He peered away from the shore. The footprints disappeared into the heather and brambles. Hemmy slipped off her knapsack, removed a bag of Plaster of Paris and made a mould of the print.

Eli flattened the ground to set up the large camera, loaded it, wound its clockwork mechanism and drew up the pendulum weight.

"Look, Eli," said Hemmy.

He peered up into the sky. A hot-air balloon floated above them and drifted on the wind. There was no other movement on land or in the water, except wind-blown branches and the lapping of wavelets.

Water birds squawked and flew up from the lake. Eli turned back to the water. He scanned the loch for any movement. Something had startled the birds. Something was gliding silently under the surface of the lake.

Breathing quickly, he reached out and set the camera mechanism.

A bow wave moved rapidly towards shore, towards Hemmy. She was only a yard from the water's edge, checking the mould and packing up the Plaster of Paris, oblivious to the oncoming danger. The water churned and bubbled behind her.

"Hemmy!" he screamed.

The Kelpie rose out of the turbulent water right next to her. It reared and howled, its backwards-facing hoofs pawing the air. Its weed-maned head swung round and knocked her into the water.

Hemmy flailed and splashed. The kelpie's muzzle lunged into her chest and pushed her under.

"No!"

Eli raced to the loch, towards Hemmy. He would tear her from its grip with his bare hands if he had to.

He looked around for a weapon. There was nothing but pebbles and brambles. Something rattled in his pocket. The silver bullets! He pulled his pistol and bullets from his inside pocket, loaded and aimed.

The blast of the pistol was deafening. The smoke cleared. The beast flung up its head as it roared. Ichor dripped down its neck. Hemmy resurfaced, gripped the monster's mane and hauled herself half out of the water.

"Don't touch it!" Too late. Eli dashed into the water.

Hemmy, gasping for breath, clambered up onto the kelpie's back. She slumped on its neck.

Eli's feet slid from under him. He skidded forward.

The monster reared, turned and plunged, swimming into deeper water, taking Hemmy with it. She screamed.

"No!" Eli fell to his knees. What had McGregor said? Our Lord's name! Dear God, make her remember to say it!

A thunder-loud crack reverberated across the water. Light flashed.

The water seethed, settled, and was still. Hemmy was gone.

"Hemmy?"

He plunged into the water and searched through the chilly murk with his hands, until his lungs felt as if they would burst.

As he resurfaced, Hemmy emerged from the depths. She gasped and spluttered; stumbled as she waded towards shore.

Eli rushed to her aid. He picked her up, buried his head into her wet hair, and wept as he carried her to safety. Together, they collapsed on the scrubby grass.

The smell of sulphur stung his nose. His eyes watered.

"Thank God you're alive." He laid her gently on the ground. "Are you all right?"

"Yes." She gulped in a breath. "Are you?" Hemmy caressed his face.

"I am now." He clasped her close as he recovered his breath. "How did you...?"

"So, you remember what Mr McGregor told us?" she asked.

"The name of Our Lord." Eli nodded.

"In Latin." Hemmy nodded. "Well, it wasn't just an old wives' tale:

it worked." She sat up and stared back at the loch. "Where did it go?" she asked.

"Don't know. Back to hell, for all I care!" He kissed her, hard.

She clung to him and shivered. A chill breeze had risen.

"We must get out of these wet clothes."

Eli helped Hemmy to her feet and draped his jacket around her shoulders.

Hemmy and Eli wandered back to where they'd abandoned their gear. Hemmy wrapped the footprint mould safely for travel. Eli packed his photographic plates carefully in their box. They set off.

There was a flash of light from amongst the heather, inland. Hemmy raised a hand to shade her eyes.

"Do you have a headache?" asked Eli.

"No. There's something reflecting over there."

He bent down, lowering his eyes to a level with hers, and followed her eyeline.

Light flashed again, and vanished. Hemmy walked towards it. Eli followed.

In a small clearing, they discovered a device set upon a tripod: a polished mahogany box, with three brass lens tubes. The two smaller were set above the largest. Intermittent sunlight reflected off the etched brass.

"Take care, Eli." She grabbed Eli's hand and halted. "Don't step within its field of view."

"What is it?" he asked.

Hemmy pushed him behind her, as they approached the contraption by a circuitous route.

"It's a *Brewer-Carlisle* camera." She tapped the gold initials and the letters, *B-C mark II*, on the side of the device.

"A…?" Eli raised an eyebrow.

"Also called *The Photocaptor*. It is extremely dangerous, and very illegal. At least we know where the kelpie went."

"Where?" Eli frowned and shook his head.

"It's in here." She placed a hand on the body of the camera. "The Empire has enemies." Hemmy removed the oversized photographic plate from the camera. "Not long ago one of those enemies invented this: a camera that can capture the living soul."

"Very good." A tall, redhaired man stepped out from the brush. In his hand was a strange object: it had a grip and a barrel, like a pistol, but its muzzle ended in a dish with three narrow projections arrayed on it.

Hemmy stepped back. The strange object he held looked too much like a pistol for comfort. "You are a clever woman, Hermia Barrington," the tall man said.

"You're the irate ornithologist," Eli said. "What are you doing here?"

"Pardon?" asked Hemmy.

"I upset a birdwatcher earlier, when your horse bolted," replied Eli. "Apparently, he holds a grudge."

She eyed the birdwatcher. He looked familiar. She frowned. None of her acquaintances had red hair. She looked examined him minutely, looking for any familiar trait. His left hand! She held her breath; she'd seen those buckled fingers before. She searched through her memories. A hand clasped in a waltz. A ruby cufflink glinting. A hand tugging a black veil.

"Fox-Torrington!" she hissed.

Fox-Torrington shrugged. "If you like."

Eli brushed the still-wet hair from his face, and, dropping his hand, felt the butt of his pistol in his pocket. He'd only shot one silver bullet. Unfortunately, wet gunpowder wouldn't fire.

"You have something I want, I believe."

Fox-Torrington covered him with a pistol-like device, and chuckled.

He eyed Eli and, with a deft motion, he clicked two ampoules into place above the barrel of his pistol. Three pins projected from a concave plate at the mouth of the weapon. He shifted his aim, just a little: a wisp of steam puffed out from one of the three pins as a dart fired and buried itself in the ground less than an inch from Eli's foot.

Eli studied the dart, trying not to flinch: its stabilising end bore a clump of red and yellow fibres; it was the same type of dart as was used to drug him on the train. Torrington probably had something to do with the viaduct, too. Eli glared at him. He *would* pay.

"Now, Mrs Barrington," cooed Torrington, "You will give that plate to me. I think Mr Mills has waited for it long enough."

Hemmy tugged her ear. Her gaze sought Eli's. Her hand drifted vaguely to her brow, brushed her eye. Her eyelids fluttered.

Eli frowned. What was she up to?

Her eyes rolled upward, as though she were going to swoon. He shook his head. Hemmy had never fainted in her life.

"Elias!" Hemmy half-wailed. She slumped towards the ground.

Aha! That's what she's doing.

"No!" Torrington darted forward and lunged to catch the photographic plate before it crashed to the ground.

Eli grabbed Torrington's projectile weapon as it fell, turned it on him.

Hemmy lifted her leg and slammed the heel of her boot into Fox-Torrington's solar plexus. Air whooshed from his lungs. He toppled backwards, hit his head on the solid ground and was knocked out cold.

She shook her skirts back down, around her ankles, and grinned at Eli.

"Very nice." He grinned back as he bound Torrington's wrists.

"The high kick, or the new silk stockings?" asked Hemmy.

"Both."

He prodded Torrington with his boot. The scoundrel groaned.

"Up, sir."

Fox-Torrington struggled to his feet.

"Move." Eli motioned towards the camp with Fox-Torrington's steam dart-pistol.

Hemmy snatched the photographic plate from the grass where it had fallen from Fox-Torrington's hand.

"If we set a good pace," said Eli, "we may have this miscreant behind bars in time for tea tomorrow."

"And scones?" Hemmy licked her lips.

"And scones." He prodded Fox-Torrington in the back, urging him towards the horses, and offered her his free arm. "Definitely scones, my dear."

Their camp was as they had left it. The firepit was undisturbed and the tent was laced tight.

"Watch him," said Eli.

Hemmy took the steam pistol from Eli, and covered Fox-Torrington with it.

Eli untied one of the tent ropes and bound Fox-Torrington's feet. Eli held out his hand and Hemmy placed the pistol in it.

A shadow crept over the camp.

Hemmy shivered, and glanced upward.

"It's that balloon I saw earlier," she said.

There were several men inside its basket. One raised a shiny telescope to his eye. Another held up a megaphone. "In the name of Her Majesty's Police, stay still, all of you." The second balloonist's voice boomed across the camp.

Hemmy and Eli complied.

"Mr Barrington? Is that you?" One of the men leaned over the edge of the basket.

"Yes!" Eli raised his hand.

"You've got Fox-Torrington?" asked the man.

"Yes." Eli nodded.

"Right, sir. We'll take over from here."

The balloon descended. Two large policemen climbed out the balloon's basket and strode towards them. They apprehended Fox-Torrington.

The senior policeman approached and tipped his helmet in Hemmy's direction.

Eli examined the officer's face and smiled.

"Charles?" he queried.

Hemmy raised an eyebrow. How did he know the policeman's name?

"Actually, it's Senior Sergeant Charles Fariner, sir." Charles grinned. "I've been following this blighter for some time now."

Hemmy and Eli followed the officers to the balloon. Fox-Torrington squirmed and smiled at the taller of his captors.

"Officer, this wig's dashed itchy," he said "I don't suppose you could…?"

"You must be joking, sir," replied the officer.

Hemmy stepped up behind Fox-Torrington, grasped the wig and pulled it off his head.

He jumped and twisted to face her.

She handed the wig to the nearest policeman. After all, it was evidence.

The cool breeze ruffled Fox-Torrington's hair.

"Madam, you are an angel." He smiled.

Hemmy flinched; her upper lip twitched. She met him with a level gaze.

"It seems so, doesn't it?" she said. Did he think he was the only one who knew about disguises?

Fox-Torrington bowed.

"That's enough of that." The tall policeman ushered Fox-Torrington towards the balloon. "Let's be having you."

"Thank you, sir, ma'am." Senior Sergeant Fariner saluted the Barringtons. "We'll keep in touch."

Sunlight poured into the room. It was too warm for a fire in the Parlour this morning and, besides, Hemmy's heart felt warm and bright without it.

She glanced across at Eli. He smiled and scribbled busily at his desk.

Hemmy sighed. It was good to be home.

She gazed at the battered letter in her hand for the last time, refolded it and slid it into its envelope. She opened a drawer in her writing desk, slipped the letter into a precious bundle tied with a red ribbon and closed the drawer. She didn't need to carry it now; she would keep an eye on Eli herself on future expeditions.

Eli placed his pen in its holder, sealed his reports to the Crypto-zoological Society, and the Royal Society and rang for the footman.

The Parlour door opened immediately.

"A letter for you, sir." John entered. "And a parcel."

"Ah, thank you." Eli took the letter and opener from the silver tray.

John placed the small parcel on the table in front of him.

"See that these are posted, will you?" Eli handed the reports to John. John bowed and withdrew.

Eli read the new letter silently, and smiled.

"Hemmy, you should read this." He passed it to Hemmy. "It's from our constabulary friend, Charles Fariner."

Hemmy took the letter and curled up on the window seat.

Dear Sir and Madam,

On the 5th day of the month inst., police officers and the accused, calling himself Edward Fox-Torrington, were proceeding in the police wagon through Inverness when a disturbance of an unknown nature caused the horses to bolt.

Upon retrieval of the carriage, the constable guarding him was discovered bound, and gagged with a silk tie, wearing nothing but his woollen combination unmentionables... (Begging your pardon, ma'am.) Regretfully, the suspect was not to be found and is still at large. He is presumed to have left the country.

We assure you our efforts to bring him to justice will not cease.

Enclosed please find, one alleged kelpie's bridle.

I remain, your humble servant,

Charles Fariner,

Senior Sergeant.

Hemmy shook her head. "I wonder where, or who, he is now?"

"He's a slippery blighter," said Eli.

"Perhaps we should have new locks installed?" she asked.

"Good idea," he replied. "I'll get John to organise it tomorrow."

Hemmy stared out the window, watched the carriages rattle down the street, and wondered what puzzles would take them to their next adventure.

THE END

Acknowledgements

Thank you to fellow local authors Katie Lowe, Karen J Carlisle and Michele Knight for their wise critiques and support, and to Gemma Swain, with whom I can discuss anything, for providing motivation. Also, to Lynne Lumsden Green, my fellow QWC Writing Racers and James Bennett for their research and technical assistance.

A big thank you to Karen J Carlisle for permission to use her 'magic lantern' device, from *The Adventures of Viola Stewart*, that became the BC Mk II, The Photocaptor.

Thanks to David Carlisle and Thomas Hutchings for computer whispering, and to Thomas for the use of his name. I'd also like to thank Cheryl Douglas, the original Hemlock Soames, for inspiration.

And finally, Miss Hemlock Soames wishes to thank Lachlan, Brecon and Karen for her conception, gestation and birthing.

About the Author

SM Kemmett scribbled her first story at seven. She flirted with various careers, but her true passion is wordsmithing.

Sharon graduated from Flinders University with a BA in English and Archaeology.

She writes speculative fiction, preferring science fiction, fantasy and steampunk, and dabbles in historical fiction.

She previously volunteered as a tour-guide at the South Australian Museum. She's currently volunteering at her neighborhood library as Local History research editor.

Sharon lives in sunny Adelaide with her 'feline domestic symbiont'.

www.smkemmettwordtailor.wordpress.com